The Hard Sell

The Hard Sell

WILLIAM HAGGARD

IVES WASHBURN, INC.
New York

IVES WASHBURN, INC., *Publishers*

750 THIRD AVENUE, NEW YORK, N.Y. 10017

THE HARD SELL

COPYRIGHT © 1965 BY WILLIAM HAGGARD

FIRST AMERICAN EDITION 1966

APR 28 '66

To safeguard the new airplane that
England badly needs, Colonel Russell of
the Security Executive travels to Italy
where he meets with violence and intrigue.

Chapter One

Colonel Charles Russell of the Security Executive had been lunching with Duncan Stoddart. He had enjoyed his lunch but was
conscious that he had been stuck again. Not that Sir Duncan had
openly sought assistance, but he was a very old friend and he had
talked with the freedom which a boyhood in common made
perfectly acceptable. This was his problem and he'd be grateful if
Russell would hear him.

So Charles Russell walked back to his unpompous room and
thought. Sir Duncan was an Ulsterman and he controlled what was
still effectively a family firm. Its business was aircraft engines, and
of their size and power they were the best in the world. His problem was now to sell them, for he didn't compete with the bigger
jets. Charles Russell sighed. He knew nothing about aeroplanes but
had formed a firm opinion of the British aircraft industry. It was
fatally addicted to building the aircraft it wished to build rather
than those which it had any real chance of selling. Preposterous
flying boats which never flew and were sold a decade later to
America as scrap, over-publicized worldbeaters which mysteriously
disintegrated, and now a military aircraft of such sophistication and
complexity that those entitled to an opinion could legitimately

doubt whether its crew could reach a target under combat conditions. No doubt there had been successes too, and when they had come they hadn't been inconsiderable. But the industry didn't strike Charles Russell as a particularly well-conducted one. He was a practical and pragmatic man and he had applied a practical and pragmatic test. He'd never owned an aircraft share.

But Duncan Stoddart hadn't been interested in what he had contemptuously dismissed as prestige projects; he didn't build engines which would lift these monsters off a runway, and he had further explained that the real money lay not in the sort of aircraft which hit the headlines but in those which did not. You built some enormous liner and no airline wished to buy it, but the industry had an outrageously powerful lobby (or had had until recently) and it went into gear at once. So some unfortunate domestic airline had to buy what it couldn't operate—not fly it and show a profit. But you built a Dakota, and thirty years later its successors were still bumbling profitably over the feeder-lines of four continents.

And it looked as though the Italians had just such an aircraft. Their industry wasn't big of course, and neither government had been interested. It wouldn't be. There was a great deal of money if the project succeeded but no prestige whatever. Sir Duncan had taken a chance on it. He made medium jet engines which would perfectly suit what he believed to be a seller for at least a generation, but even with British engines SAGA wasn't big enough alone. So Sir Duncan had put his shirt on it; he'd backed them to the hilt.

And now things were going most seriously wrong. Sir Duncan had drunk some brandy thoughtfully. One didn't stumble on this sort of project by accident: it meant research, cost analysis, above all the most careful tailoring to what the market would want and take. Which inevitably implied that others could do what you were, and it was common knowledge that another aircraft industry

2

was something more than interested. So it came down in the end to a question of time. Get your aircraft flying first, and if you hadn't misread the market there'd be a queue for your order book. But get it flying only second and you were simply another competitor.

So you couldn't accept what was happening at Vittorio—the administrative misjudgements, the minor mishaps, a whole series of incidents which could be explained as bad luck but which Sir Duncan didn't think so. They simply couldn't afford the delay.

He had risen a little abruptly. Well, there it was. It had been courteous of Russell to listen to him. There was a plane back to Belfast and he must catch it.

Back in his room Charles Russell thought for half an hour, then spoke to his secretary. She was to cancel his engagements for as far ahead as possible and to book him a seat on the morning flight to Vittorio. The bill was to be sent to him personally.

Russell could have found a dozen reasons for charging his trip to the taxpayer but he wouldn't have been offended to be called old-fashioned. Which meant in turn that he was unfashionably scrupulous. This wasn't Executive business.

Charles Russell smiled, for he had experience of private chores which unaccountably exploded into politics. So this wasn't Executive business, or not yet.

Now he was in the car which Neil Stoddart had brought to the airport at Vittorio. He was Duncan Stoddart's son but Russell hadn't seen him for several years. He was on the board of the company, which guaranteed competence, for Stoddart's weren't the sort of firm where even a son would have been accepted as a director if he'd been wholly inefficient. But he was still in his early thirties and this was his first big job alone. His father had been frank about it: he was a competent boy and Sir Duncan trusted him, but if there really were more than met the eye he wouldn't carry the guns for it.

(Quite so, Russell thought, or we shouldn't be lunching.)

They drove slowly through the winter fog, Vittorio's fog which made London's seem innocuous. Neil Stoddart said politely: 'It was kind of you to come, sir.'

'But I'm promising you nothing.'

'Father made that clear but still you've come. I thought I'd introduce you first to Doctor Franchin. He's managing director of the aircraft division of SAGA but he hasn't a seat on the main board yet.' Neil Stoddart smiled. 'Now if he'd married into the family. . . .' He left it unfinished. 'And I've a seat on the aircraft company myself—that was part of the bargain with my father. You could say that SAGA is building the aircraft for us to engine her. Of course I've a say in the designing too, but basically I'm the engines-man.' Neil Stoddart looked at Russell. 'And you can't put your engines into a plane which doesn't exist.'

'It's getting as bad as that, then?'

'Not quite. But if we don't have her flying in a matter of weeks we're going to lose the cream of it.'

'You're talking of the prototype?'

'Yes, but much more. This isn't another Concord but a perfectly viable medium-haul commercial aircraft. It's no good just having a prototype if that's the market you're going for. So there's a production line almost finished and it cost us a lot of money. Some was the firm's but more was just Father's. He's a very determined man. He's got a heart, by the way, and I'm afraid this might finish him.'

'I didn't know that.'

They turned past what had once been the lodge of a country villa, going slowly along the drive, now metalled and the main artery of the factory. On either side the huge hangars of the aircraft industry loomed through the blanketing fog. It was surprisingly quiet, the world of the moving car unnaturally isolated in what Russell knew was a considerable establishment. They drew up at the villa, now evidently offices, and both men got out. Stoddart said in explanation: 'We're a bit outside the main industrial area, though it's creeping out on us. It suits us though, since we have to have an airstrip. We run buses for the workers and we're as paternal as we can be. That makes it all the harder to understand when....'

'Yes?' Russell said.

But Stoddart didn't answer. They walked up the curving garden stairs and Russell was looking at a villa in the Lombard style he deprecated. Longhena, in the Veneto, would have done it much better. They took an unnecessary lift to what had been the *piano nobile*, Stoddart opening the door into a room which ran the villa's length. It was a fine room still despite its tiresome ornament, though the wall on one whole side had been replaced by modern glass. A man behind an important desk rose instantly, and Stoddart introduced him. 'Doctor Angelo Franchin—Colonel Charles Russell.'

Russell shook hands and inspected Franchin. He was a man of forty-five or so, almost a stereotype of the prosperous northern Italian business man. He was no longer thin but he wasn't yet gross; his sleek hair was black and he still had all of it; he wore elegant spectacles and a tie which you wouldn't notice in a shirt by Caleffi. He said now pleasantly: 'It was good of you to come. At short notice, I gather.'

'You speak very good English.'

'I spent a year in England. Will you have a cigar?'

After a second's hesitation Russell took one, and he was lighting it carefully when inexplicably the match blew out. A blast rocked his chair but he didn't quite fall. The next thing he knew was the shocking crash of glass. He ducked instinctively, and when he looked up again the fog was drifting in on them. The bang came an instant later.

Franchin was on his feet at once, crunching the window's debris as he walked to where it had been. Outside there were fog and

5

shouting men. The lights had gone out but now came on again. Neil Stoddart said: 'Second circuit, that,' and Doctor Franchin: 'Good God.'

He came back to his desk as the telephone rang peremptorily, picking it up and listening, still standing. At length he said: 'The hydraulics, they think. It's blown all the presses but there's no sign of a fire yet.' He listened again. 'And they've caught a young man——'

'Bring him here,' Stoddart said.

'But. . . .'

Charles Russell turned his head an inch, watching Franchin without appearing to. The Doctor's 'but' had caught his ear, the unmistakable tone of an indecision. But they'd caught a man—good luck to them—so why not bring him up at once?

Russell said politely: 'I think we should have a look at him.' This was going to be interesting.

Doctor Angelo shrugged, sat down. The three men waited.

The youth they brought in was not impressive—loose-mouthed, hands working, more than a little frightened. Four men stood round him but now they weren't holding him. One was older than the others, wearing the row of fountain pens in the breast pocket of white overalls which in SAGA was a supervisor's badge of rank. Doctor Angelo spoke to him: 'Signor Pasquale?'

'It was some sort of bomb, sir, but not well placed. Not—not clever. But it's killed the whole pressure system.'

'How long to repair?' Neil Stoddart asked.

'Three days perhaps.'

'That might be worse but only just.'

Franchin had interrupted them, nodding sideways at the shaking boy, not meeting his eyes directly. 'Who's this?'

'He won't give his name but he's not one of ours. He hasn't a pass and nobody knows him. That's why we grabbed him.'

'Was he running away?'

6

'No, he was wandering—shocked, I should say. It was really quite a bang if you happened to be close to it.'

'Look at those windows.' The Dottore considered. 'He hadn't papers on him—nothing?'

'Nothing at all, sir.'

Franchin swung round on the trembling boy. 'And what's your accursed name?' he asked.

The youth stared at him dully and Franchin rose; he picked up a ruler. It was an ebony ruler, round and two feet long.

Russell said: 'Steady,' and Franchin sat down again. Russell was puzzled. He knew about Italians, they loved melodrama as they loved their lives, but it was his impression that even by Italian standards Franchin was overplaying it. And had he caught the oddest glance between the boy and the director? He spoke to Neil Stoddart but he was watching Franchin still. 'Then we'd better call the police.'

'The police! But this isn't England.' Franchin had barked it.

'Quite. But you've an excellent Commissario and I'm in duty bound to call on him tomorrow before I leave.'

'You're leaving tomorrow?'

'I was *hoping* to leave tomorrow.'

'I see. I'm sorry. I——'

But Neil Stoddart was saying quietly: 'I agree about the police.' He telephoned and Franchin watched him. Charles Russell was watching Franchin. He'd made two slips (but were they slips?) but now he was smooth as oil again. Charles Russell rose as Stoddart finished. He declined the offer of escort to his hotel, but if he could use Neil Stoddart's car. . . ? He'd ring him tomorrow when the incident was clearer. This wasn't his territory and he couldn't interfere on it.

He climbed into his car reflectively, giving the driver the address of his hotel. He had made the booking personally, for Russell knew Vittorio. Its hotels could be extravagant or they could simply be uncomfortable. This one was neither and its food was to Russell's taste.

He lit one of his own cigars and thought. He thought very hard for the seven miles back to Vittorio.

*

The Commissario Mario Donnini was in an indifferent temper, for like all good policemen his idea of the perfect day was the day on which nothing happened. And today something had. More precisely he had received a telegram of great courtesy and in passable Italian from a Colonel Charles Russell of the British Security Executive. Russell was coming to Vittorio on private business but naturally he would do himself the honour of calling on Mario Donnini. The Commissario frowned. He had never met Charles Russell but he had heard of him—oh certainly he'd heard of him—and he could make something better than a guess at the reason for Russell's visit. It would be this new aeroplane at SAGA, the one which the British were backing. Donnini knew all about the scheme and it hadn't been going as well as it might. It hadn't indeed. There had been a series of setbacks, none of them singly disastrous, but in total rather more than a sensible man could accept as coincidence. Nor did Mario Donnini do so. He had his own explanation and it was reasonable: for some motive he hadn't rumbled yet the communists were against the thing; they had decided that the *Princess Rose* should never fly, and in Vittorio and perhaps elsewhere they had power to effect just that. Not through the unions—they despised them the more as they infiltrated steadily —but through their own key men, the cells, the formidable organization which, if they wished it, could bring SAGA to a standstill in an hour. But unemployment might not suit their book and they had certainly other methods.

Donnini frowned again as the telephone rang, then swore softly

8

as he listened to it. Nothing could be more disastrously timed. For one thing they hadn't before ventured overt sabotage, and to choose the day of this Russell's arrival. . . .

Explosives at that. They were getting impertinent.

He said that he would come at once but instead sat quietly thinking. They'd caught some wretched boy, it seemed, and Donnini knew what that meant. The boy would break. He'd implicate his masters and that was that.

For Donnini that might be that indeed, for he had just exiled from the city a newly arrived but powerful communist.

Who happened to be his cousin. Their relationship wasn't known yet and if the cousin behaved himself perhaps it never need be. But the first foot put wrong and Donnini would be finished. No Commissario owned an activist communist cousin and kept his job. The Commissario smiled wryly. Not that cousin was quite the proper word, they hadn't a drop of common blood, but Donnini's mother had had a sister and this sister had married a man called Dagrappi. Dagrappi in turn had a brother with sons and the eldest had been Renato. Donnini drew it out on his scribbling pad, then carefully destroyed it. Renato Dagrappi was the son of his aunt's brother-in-law. In Italy that was quite a close relationship, and in Sicily it was practically a brother.

Like many senior policemen Donnini was a Sicilian—a Sicilian on the naked horns. Well, wriggling wouldn't help him.

He picked up the telephone and spoke into it softly. He had changed his mind about coming out to SAGA. There was nothing he could do there which his subordinates could not, but the boy was to be brought to headquarters immediately. Unmindful of the opera he loved he added matter-of-factly: 'Apply the normal pressure.'

Chapter Two

Charles Russell had left London without finishing his homework, the basic research without which no sensible officer started on an assignment, but he had left instructions that the papers should be flown down to him and he was reading them in Vittorio with his coffee next morning. It was a fair-sized file, since Vittorio was an important city, more than important enough for the Executive to keep a stringer there. Ostensibly he was the correspondent of an international news agency, and as far as it went quite genuinely, but he reported as well to the Security Executive. Russell began on a well-informed précis of communist influence in Vittorio. This he knew already but he read it again quickly, then turned to the rest. It began with an appreciation of the social and economic situation in the city, and this he studied carefully. He knew little of economics but he was good at getting the smell of things, and the smell of Vittorio was one of a startling but not particularly secure prosperity. Certainly there had been an economic miracle, but what went up came down again and often very down indeed. Labour relations were a good deal past the stage of the brutal exploitation which foreigners often assumed they were, but you could call them paternalistic—Neil Stoddart himself had used the word—and already there were the stirrings of unease. All this was a communist paradise.

Charles Russell read this thoroughly twice, then moved to the final section, thumbnail sketches of Vittorians who might interest him. There was one of the Professor, the real power behind SAGA, and another of Commissario Mario Donnini. The Security Executive had a high opinion of Mario Donnini. He was ambitious and efficient, a very good man in a notoriously difficult post, for Vittorio wasn't a city where the niceties of the legal system were regarded with an Anglo-Saxon deference. Plenty of big boys had plenty of protection and the despised, the almost alien government in Rome was apt to be interfering in little local difficulties which it didn't understand. Especially when it was prompted to. So that the job of Vittorio's head of police wasn't a policeman's feather bed. But Donnini seemed to enjoy it, and it was a safe generalization that a policeman who enjoyed his job would usually do it well. Of course he was a Sicilian with the defects of his blood as well as its advantages, a certain fondness for an almost abstract Machiavellianism, intrigue to meet a taste for it and not because it served a concrete end. But the Executive's assessment of Mario Donnini was still that he was a good one.

Russell looked at the last three single sheets. They were names he had never heard of and there wasn't much about them, but this didn't surprise him. It was legitimate that the Executive should have an adequate assessment of the political situation in Vittorio, for politics were indivisible, especially communist politics, but it was no part of its business to hold dossiers on such Vittorians as might worry the local police. Nor were these papers dossiers. They were the names of three men who might conceivably be interesting, but only one of them pricked attention. It was Luthman, Carl Luthman, a Swede. He had lived in Vittorio for twenty-five years but he hadn't changed nationality. He had an import-export business, mostly import, and he went shopping in America at least twice a year. Naturally he had contacts there. None had excited interest until recently, when a man was known to have called on him whose movements were of almost hourly concern to certain retiring Americans. They'd reported back to the Executive because this man had once been British. Russell had useful friends and valued them.

He put the file in his briefcase and looked at his watch. His appointment with Mario Donnini was at half-past ten, and he bathed and shaved leisurely.

The Commissario received him with a manner which Russell approved. He wasn't effusive but he wasn't suspicious either. Russell was a colleague, a colleague of great distinction, and he was entitled to normal courtesies. Anything more would simply have put his back up. Donnini's welcome might almost have been English, and certainly he spoke it well. Over coffee he said amiably: 'I can guess what brought you down here.'

'Of course. I'd have told you in any case. It's this trouble at SAGA.'

'A very bad business.'

'Business is the proper word. We've a terrible lot of money sunk in the *Princess Rose*.'

'A delightful name for an aeroplane, isn't it? So—so English.'

'I'd call it a selling title.'

'I beg your pardon?'

Charles Russell let it go but went on smoothly. 'I'm not here officially but you already know that. Sir Duncan Stoddart is a very old friend and he told me his troubles. So I thought I'd come and pick your brains.'

'You flatter me. There's been more than ordinary delay in the production schedule of this aircraft, more than enough to raise suspicion, but up to yesterday afternoon there'd been nothing you could put your finger on. Then Colonel Charles Russell flies down here from London and somebody bombs the factory.' The Commissario considered. 'You think the two were connected?'

'I should very much doubt it.'

'Frankly, so should I, but if you took only the *local* timing. . . . Assuming that somebody is interested in delaying the *Princess Rose*. . . .' Donnini looked at Russell. 'We *may* assume that?'

'We are.'

'Then whoever was delaying was behind *his* schedule—the delay was insufficient. So he moves into open sabotage. He *has* to.'

Russell said quietly: 'They caught some young man.'

'We're interrogating him now and you'll know what will happen. He'll break—they always do.' Donnini spoke without relish and almost with regret. Russell saw that he wasn't a vicious man, only too sensible to attempt to change a system.

'Implicating whom?'

'The next man in line in the communist chain—that's the only one he'll know about. They learnt that in the Resistance and it's thoroughly sound practice.'

'Who may not lead you to the principals?'

' I doubt it.' Donnini might have added but did not: 'I hope it.'

Charles Russell rose. 'I leave it on your plate, then. In any case I can do nothing.'

'But I think you might.'

Russell sat down again. 'Yes?'

'I'd have a word with your man, George Bailey. We hold him quite highly here.'

Russell wasn't surprised and he was far from offended. He had a stringer in Vittorio and Donnini seemed to know of him. That, if it was anything, was simply reassuring. These Italian police were competent. Russell said blandly: 'I'll take your advice. And when I get back to London may I convey your compliments to the head waiter at the Magnificent?'

'Yes please, do that.'

13

The two men laughed.

Charles Russell rose again and Mario Donnini walked to the door with him. At it, he asked politely: 'Shall we meet again?'

'I'm booked on the evening flight, you know.'

'But may not go?'

'That depends on George Bailey. Remember, he was your idea.'

'*D'accordo.*'

'Are you sure you don't mind my talking to Bailey?'

The Commissario bowed. 'Rashness,' he said, 'isn't part of your reputation.'

When Russell had gone Donnini sat down again. He drew from a drawer a report on an all-night interrogation of a frightened but stubborn young man. Nothing was conclusive yet, but though Donnini hadn't interfered in the interrogation he had looked at the youth and weighed him. This boy was a layabout, an unfortunate from some broken home, a mile away from serious crime and quite unfitted to attempt it. He'd have convictions for theft but hardly sabotage. Vittorio's communists were a serious political party and it was difficult to believe that they'd employ a petty criminal on a job of half-baked violence. But it wasn't yet proved they hadn't, and when they broke this wretch's peasant stubbornness. . . .

He might break Donnini too, and quite irreparably. He'd know only the next man in the communist ladder, but ladders led upwards, the police must try to climb the rungs, and Donnini had a cousin called Renato Dagrappi.

Donnini couldn't risk it. He looked at his handsome clock, since he had a decision to make and he had to get the timing right. He couldn't call off an interrogation prematurely; he couldn't without suspicion. But after twenty-four hours it was standard practice to relax a little—a meal, cigarettes, even sleep, though not too much of it. Donnini looked at the clock again. The boy had been brought in at three in the afternoon the day before and it was now past eleven. That was three or four hours short of what was normal, but

Donnini decided that he must chance it. He picked up the telephone and gave crisp, decided orders. 'Lay off him for a bit,' he said. 'Lay off him till I tell you.'

He put back the telephone and began to pace his room. He was a policeman on a dangerous spot but he'd been there before and he was still the Commissario. And he hadn't been wholly stupid. It had been uncovenanted good fortune that this Russell had come flying in and Donnini had promptly seized it. He hadn't choked Charles Russell off, he'd given him a come-on. That wasn't a plan or even the beginnings of one but it was perfectly sound in principle. Englishmen existed to be used by more gifted Latins, and when one's motives had something in common, on Russell's side that this distressingly-named aircraft should fly on schedule, and on his own that it should do so without losing him his career. . . .

Donnini had no idea what Russell would do, but he had a formidable reputation, in his way he was a sort of myth, and for Mario Donnini that was enough. He rubbed his hands contentedly. This was a complicated situation so one made it a little more so. Then one seized one's advantages as lesser men offered them.

That was sound southern thinking.

Charles Russell took a taxi from the *questura* back to his hotel. His thoughts weren't southern or even thoughts. Pressed by his peers he would have admitted that he wasn't really thinking. He was a man of potent instincts which he trusted and mistrusted equally. But he trusted them when they really clicked and now they were signalling strongly.

There was something in this *questura* and the something smelt to heaven.

*

Doctor Franchin hadn't slept all night for Doctor Franchin was frightened. The luck was turning against him and he knew it. He had accepted a bribe from Luthman with his eyes open, but he had rationalized the acceptance. He had heard a cliché in England, 'social justice', and it had somehow stayed his conscience. It wasn't social justice that the Family should take so much while he himself, a technocrat, a man of a competence which he didn't trouble to conceal, was merely paid a salary. Admittedly it was a good one but SAGA was the Family, Montis to a man of them, Montis born and Montis married, uncles and cousins and sons and brides unto the third and fourth generation of the least little Monti. The Professor was their tribal chief and a very shrewd old gentleman. He knew which Monti was worth his salt and he put him to work accordingly. The rest he pensioned ruthlessly since that cost the firm far less money. A Monti of the second class sailed grandly at Portofino or, if the fancy took him, cut a figure on his allowance in the international set in Rome. The Professor despised both equally, but neither was relevant to the economics of SAGA. Only good Montis worked there.

But if as sometimes happened he couldn't find one qualified the Professor would look outside. Angelo Franchin was an example. The Professor had spotted him as an outstanding designer of aircraft; he had nursed him and promoted him; he paid him very handsomely. But Franchin wasn't satisfied. He was very well paid but that was all; he hadn't a lira of the equity.

Not, he thought sourly, that he couldn't have had it. At a price, very naturally, and the price was determined: you married a Monti. Indeed it had even been indicated to him which lady of the Monti clan might not find his advances distasteful. Franchin was an Italian, and in the serious business of marriage it hadn't worried him excessively that the lady was older than himself and moreover was having trouble with a moustache a good deal stronger than his own: what had worried him was that she wasn't particularly senior in the clan. She had fifty thousand pounds perhaps, and in the vast Monti empire fifty thousand was simply chickenfeed.

Angelo hadn't followed up.

And at once things had started to go wrong for him. Nothing outrageous—that wasn't Monti form at all. He was already managing director of the aircraft division and there hadn't been even a whisper that he should do otherwise than remain so, but he'd had reasonably-founded hopes of a seat on the main board itself. They'd collapsed ignominiously—ignominiously because when a vacancy at last occurred the man selected had been both Franchin's junior and, in his own view, notably his inferior. But he was safely married to a Monti. And Franchin had been expecting a rise in salary. He had received it too—half what he'd been hoping for.

So he'd been decidedly anti-Monti when he'd met Carl Luthman. The Swede had been living with the divorced wife of one of the uncounted Monti agnates. Her marriage had been annulled and she'd resented it. She'd played her wedding cool, of course— played it modern Italian. Not a bride of any sophistication who, going happily to the altar, did not call her bridesmaids aside and throw a highstrike. . . . 'I don't want to marry him, my parents are making me, *forcing* me. . . .' That was evidence which the Roman wheels could grind on if later it came to it, an insurance which cost nothing and which it would be un-Italian to neglect.

The lady hadn't resented that this poor little farce had been turned against her since that was a risk which she couldn't have avoided. But there had been a much better reason for annulment and she'd been tricked into misplaying it. The marriage had never been consummated, and for a reason which in any country north of the Alps or Pyrenees would have given her a divorce against her husband out of hand. But the Montis had been horrified. . . . But she couldn't use *that*! The marriage hadn't been consummated— let it simply go at that. She had shut her mouth on the promise of a generous settlement.

She hadn't received it.

The lady and Luthman had worked on Franchin cleverly, playing on his conceit, above all on a deeply-felt sense of injustice. Why, the aircraft division would fall to pieces tomorrow if Franchin weren't there to prop it up. It was an outrage that this enormous clan, playboys, *figli di papa*, should control the greatest industrial empire in southern Europe while the men who really ran it were their servants. Finally they played their trump. It was revenge, not quite naked, but revenge just the same. It was a duty to teach these industrialists a lesson.

It had turned the trick but only just, for Franchin's roots were in SAGA and he didn't intend to cut them. He had built the aircraft division from something which made flyabouts for rich Italian playboys into a serious industry capable of building a *Princess Rose*. She was his creature, his child, though not his favourite. His favourite lay in a drawer of his desk. The Professor's unspoken opinion of him was that he was a designer of near-genius, and it was an opinion which Franchin would never have questioned privately. He hadn't the least intention of destroying his own prospects, especially with those plans in his desk, another and bigger aircraft, a splendid thing, a lifetime's dream. But a few months' delay would damage nothing but Monti pockets. And that he'd felt entitled to.

Especially when he could line his own. Doctor Franchin had once been poor and the offer they'd made had staggered him. He'd accepted a hundred thousand—more to come. A hundred thousand dollars. Cash.

And now he was regretting it for the whole thing was out of hand. He'd been told that there was no particular hurry, that a gentle slowing-down over the next six months would be all that would be required of him, the sort of thing which any administrator of his competence could contrive without implicating himself. He'd been shattered when Luthman had demanded immediate, desperate action. At first he had refused, for this wasn't their bargain, but he wasn't the first man to find himself holding the awkward end of the traditional blackmail stick. He'd taken Luthman's money and the Swede had him helpless. . . . Then how was he to operate? He knew nothing of sabotage, he hadn't the skills or tools.

Luthman had shrugged but put a briefcase on the table. That was what he'd *paid* for.

And everything had gone wrong again. He couldn't have done the plant himself and somehow he hadn't wished to, but his connection with the world of criminals had been tenuous in the extreme. Even that wretched boy he'd stumbled on in a bar. He'd been very poor material but Franchin had lacked alternatives. And it had seemed simple enough. Nip in on the midday shift and make the plant. Set the fuse—Franchin had shown him. Hide. Nip out when the whistle went.

Instead he'd made a mess of it, mis-setting the fuse, shocking himself and getting caught. This English Colonel had come flying down. . . .

Doctor Angelo reviewed his position. Run for it, leave the country? Yes, that might still be possible, but there was one thing against it: he'd lost the hundred grand when the market had collapsed on him. He'd gone in at the top with his first big money. Go to the police? But this was Vittorio. They'd not only prosecute but they'd hang on him every petty crime in SAGA for a generation back. Go to the Professor, then—throw yourself on his mercy? But the Professor wasn't that sort of man.

And that boy, Doctor Angelo thought again. He'd demanded his name when they'd dragged him in yesterday since it wouldn't have looked natural if he hadn't. But he'd been terrified that he'd blurt it out there and then. . . . 'You know who I am. You gave me money, told me. . . .' The little comedy he'd played hadn't satisfied that Englishman. In any case there was still the boy: the police would break him at their leisure. That was the just word for it. If they really turned the heat on him they'd break him in an hour but if they played it *adagio* he might last perhaps half a day more. He hadn't much motive not to.

The half of a day, that meant till noon.

Angelo Franchin thought with his mouth open but now his teeth snapped suddenly. He was a bought Italian but he wasn't a coward. He'd stick and he'd see it out.

He dragged himself up to SAGA.

*

The Baron Renato Dagrappi never used his title. For one thing he was a communist and he disapproved of titles, and for another he was a man of the world and perfectly aware that penniless Sicilian barons were six a dollar among the beach-boys. Nevertheless he received his cousin the Commissario when he called on him that evening with a certain antique reserve.

In a sense he had been expecting him. After all the flat was Mario's, the weekend hideout at Rapallo which a successful citizen of Vittorio would consider he owed himself, and Maria had used it as final sweetener in the complicated Sicilian game of squeeze and counter-squeeze by which the Commissario had successfully and quite without recourse to law obliged a newly-arrived but potentially dangerous communist to take himself off at pleasure. Pleasure, in this case, had meant simply till the balance broke, till Dagrappi found the extra weight to tilt the beam back in his favour. It might be almost anything, some foolish excess by a sergeant of *carabinieri*, some municipal contract which Mario Donnini was taking his cut on. Renato Dagrappi would hear of both, for he had very good sources indeed. But the Commissario valued silence and in either of these cases he should have it. The price would be simple—Renato's return to Vittorio. Not a word need be spoken, and the bargain implicit would be most

20

scrupulously kept. Both men knew the rules and neither wished to change them.

And Renato Dagrappi had another reason for expecting a call from his cousin. He hadn't been using the telephone which he rightly assumed to be tapped, but he'd been reading the newspapers, reading between the lines. And there'd been an incident at SAGA. The newspapers had been handling it remarkably cagily, but this wasn't the first time the Press had soft-pedalled SAGA. One thing was clear, though: there'd been an explosion in the aircraft plant and this Anglo-Italian aircraft would be delayed once again. Any fool could add two and two, no doubt. Renato made them five.

So he received the Commissario with politeness but with ceremony, offering him a glass of his own whisky before Donnini could reach the sideboard. 'Did you motor?' Renato asked.

'Of course.'

'I'm really very comfortable here, I'm rather enjoying my exile. By the way, where's Maria?'

Donnini said stiffly: 'The signorina has returned to her *paese*.'

'Temporarily, I hope—for the duration of my visit.' He was teasing the police and enjoying it. 'Never mind, I get on splendidly alone.'

'You're my guest,' Donnini said.

'But I don't much like the sound of that. Guests have obligations and hosts sometimes trade on them.'

'You could do me a favour, I don't deny it.'

'I'm not stopping you asking. I've a very good reason to get back to Vittorio soon. So a small *combinazione*——'

'We'll see.' Donnini sat down with his whisky, waving at the crumpled newspapers. 'That business at SAGA——'

Renato exploded. 'Good God, be your age. You can't think we had a hand in that. We've better things to do by far.'

The Commissario considered him. He would gladly have seen

Renato dead, but he had known him since childhood and he had all of a policeman's instinct for the truth. Besides, it sounded credible. His own impression had already been that if that boy was a communist he'd give up coffee for a week. But he had a card still and he played it, watching his cousin across his drink. 'Now this isn't in the papers yet but we picked up a man at SAGA, *colto in flagrante*, a petty crook of maybe twenty.'

He thought for a moment Renato would strike him. Instead he said icily: 'We don't use teenage crooks, you know.'

'I beg your pardon.' Donnini had made his mind up and he hadn't found it difficult; he went on without change of tone. 'So I've come here to ask your help.'

'I sometimes sell it.'

'Good. Then accepting that you haven't been bombing SAGA you could stop further nonsense in a day if you decided to. Whether it's you or somebody else it's still an embarrassment to a Commissario of police to have SAGA played the fool with. A man flew down yesterday from England, a Colonel Charles Russell of the Security Executive——'

'I've heard of it. And him.'

'Help a kinsman in a jam then.'

Renato thought it over, at last saying non-committally: 'I don't deny that we have resources inside SAGA which could help you. You can guess what they can do and what they can't, and you wouldn't believe me if I told you they couldn't police the thing. A word in a couple of dozen ears and I wouldn't give much for further sabotage.' Dagrappi thought again. 'And what are you offering?'

'You know Neil Stoddart, don't you?'

'I do. He's a competent engineer, or so they tell me, but he's not too much else. Except a marvellous golfer. That's how I met him. Golf's a snob game in Italy and I shouldn't be playing it, but I need my exercise and frankly I enjoy it. So I went out to the club one day without a game, and there was this Stoddart on the putting green. I knew he was good, I couldn't ask him, but he walked straight up, gave an English bow, and proposed himself as a partner. I told him I was Twenty-four but he said that didn't matter. By God, he's good. He shoots in the high seventies, better when he's trying, but he didn't mind what I did. I lost a couple of balls and I picked up twice, but he didn't turn a hair. That—that's *courteous*. And you'll hardly believe it but when we got back he asked me to play again. An Italian of Four or better would have died before he'd play again.'

'And did you?'

'Yes.'

'Free lessons?'

'Naturally.'

'Then you might consider repaying him.'

'By helping him out at SAGA? Come off it. He's a very pleasant Englishman. Englishmen of that class are. They're well-mannered and that's the lot of them.' Dagrappi leant forward. 'I told you I sometimes sold,' he said. 'I sell our help but I never give it.'

'I'm ready to negotiate.'

'I'm not. I want to get back to Vittorio—now.'

'That's an ultimatum, not a starting price.'

'I haven't got a starting price. I want to get back. I *must*.'

'If you'd care to explain——'

'You know I can't.'

'Of course not—a silly question.' The Commissario shook his head; he shook it reluctantly but still he shook it. 'I'm not ready for your return just yet, or not without undertakings.'

'No undertakings. Take it or leave it.'

'I'm sorry.' Donnini sounded it. 'You're bouncing me far too high.'

'You leave it?'

'I leave.'

'So be it.' Renato rose. 'May I offer another whisky?'

'My own excellent whisky which I acquire from you-know-where? It's so very much cheaper.' Donnini drank, looking at the bottle. It was empty. He struggled silently, finally surrendered. The obligations of hospitality were inescapable. He spoke without enthusiasm but he spoke.

'There's a crate in the cellar.'

Renato Dagrappi laughed at him. 'Cousin,' he said, 'I've already found it.'

Chapter Three

The Commissario Donnini had motored to Rapallo but the head of the Security Executive had stayed quietly in Vittorio. He had telephoned to George Bailey, who had clearly been shocked by the open call since it wasn't the Executive's policy to tell its stringers that the local police, if competent, could be expected to have a file on them. Russell had said simply that he was staying at the Manin under his own name and that the matter was fairly urgent. He would be grateful for Bailey's company at dinner at eight o'clock. The food was good.

Russell rang down to the restaurant, ordering carefully, then he put on his hat and overcoat. He had three hours to kill and he needed exercise.

He told his taxi to drive north-west, stopping it in the heart of the industrial area. Then he began to walk, erect and lean, sixty but not looking it—scarf, beautiful gloves and walking stick, inescapably English and in no way ashamed of it. He wasn't interested in the factories but in the people around him. There were stark blocks of flats, but Russell preferred them to the cat-infested gardens of a broken-down suburbia. The fog had thinned and he could see washing on balconies. Women shouted from them lustily in every dialect of their native south, apparently quarrelling seriously but Russell knew better. One of them seemed to be calling to him. He couldn't understand a word but he took off his hat politely. Unnumbered children, invariably well cared for, played in the crowded streets. There were cafés and men inside them. They were playing *scopa*, or a mysterious form of billiards which Russell had tried to learn and failed. There was a casual, thriving street market, and at a corner what seemed to be a political meeting. Charles Russell stopped and listened. His Italian was serviceable but again he couldn't catch a word. He went into a bar and drank. The waiter, politely but with unfeigned curiosity, asked him where he came from. 'From London,' he said. Ah, London—what a city! The taxes were absurdly high and moreover one had to pay them. Not like in Vittorio. More than one Italian had been bitterly disappointed, but still one could make a living there, do well when one knew the ropes.

All this in a Tuscan as unnatural as a uniform, fishing for the words learnt at school.

They chatted for half an hour, then Russell rose. He walked into what was now the night, but the life in the streets had not abated. Rather it had intensified. The precocious children swarmed and yelled, and the women were on parade by now, the young ones. They walked demurely in twos and threes, arms linked, dressed with a simple elegance which they drew from God knew where, *commessa*, stenographer, as sharp as pins, perfectly aware of the men's long glances which they would have died before acknowledging. The men leant in doorways, not always with overcoats in a cold which made Russell shiver. They watched the girls but they did not accost them. This was a ritual, descended from antiquity. It had its own firm rules and an old, established discipline. Life—life in the streets, the life of a people who lived it with simple gusto.

Russell found himself remembering the bad lands. When work would allow it he golfed at weekends and he took the train to

26

Sunningdale to do so. Whitton, he thought, and Feltham too, the gravel pits, the Borstal.

A desert.

He checked himself quickly for that wasn't quite fair. The English weren't the only people who ravished themselves in lonely suburban dormitories. Only an hour's drive to the south-east a powerful Italian industrialist had had his *folie de grandeur*. He had hired an eminent architect and told him to please himself. What had emerged had been the city of the future, detached little houses and beautiful lawns and gardens. There was even a civic centre. Charles Russell smiled. It had been impressive if you liked it, but for the industrialist it hadn't been quite successful. For this splendid modern company town dragged one serious disadvantage.

The workers wouldn't stay in it.

Charles Russell smiled again, looking round for a taxi. He wasn't surprised there wasn't one, and he took a bus happily. The driver could understand him but only just. Yes, they went to the centre and somewhere near via Manin. Russell settled and smoked. A notice told him not to but he wasn't quite a stranger. Everyone else was smoking comfortably. They seemed to be going a long way round and Russell looked at his watch. He was going to be late and in England he would have fretted. Here he chatted to a stout neighbour and in no time knew all about her. She had a grandson in hospital and another in prison. It was a disaster of course, but it didn't seem insupportable. Nothing was that. Russell recognized a landmark and got out. Here there were taxis and he took one. He'd never felt more relaxed.

George Bailey was waiting for him in the hall and Russell apologized. They went straight to their table. Russell hadn't yet met Bailey and he seemed a little younger than he'd expected. That might be an advantage. The first duty of a stringer was to report what was interesting but at a pinch they could have others. Russell said pleasantly: 'It's a complicated business.'

'You mean what goes on at SAGA, sir? Yes, it is. Up to yesterday there'd been a series of minor delays, none of them sensational individually, but collectively looking more than a little odd. That's an understatement if you think it so, but six black rabbits aren't one black hare. But yesterday somebody bombs the place and that's sabotage in six languages.'

'Would you care to guess who did it?'

George Bailey shook his head.

'It could have been the communists?'

'It could but I rather doubt it. It wouldn't fit. The economy has been booming here but now it's begun to crack a bit. The market's gone down by sixty per cent and a good many people were caught in it. It hit the building industry first as it always does, and there's a good deal of unemployment. Then the engineering industries, cars and the rest of them, the backbone really, went over to short-time working. I'm not an expert on the theory of communism but I know some of the very practical citizens who run it here, and I doubt whether any practical communist would choose the middle of a quite serious slump to lumber the faithful with more unemployment.'

'In any case, if they'd wanted to shut down SAGA couldn't they have done it without sabotage?'

'I'm sure of it.'

Russell reflected. 'Have you a private line on it?'

'I haven't.'

'No more have we. But they sent me a file this morning, so for the little it's worth let's check it. They sent me three names and I'm wondering if you've heard of them . . . Pasquale Massaro?'

'I've seen the name in the newspapers. He's a supervisor at SAGA and influential in what's still the biggest union in Vittorio. He has a reputation for ambition.'

'All we know of him at our end is that he once applied for a job in England. I gather he's not a communist?'

'He's emphatically anti-communist. So is his union.'

Russell looked at his second paper. 'Fred Adams, then?'

George Bailey laughed. 'I've met Fred Adams. He's an expatriate Englishman of a recognizable type. He wrote a successful novel in the 'thirties, then decided he'd shake the dust off. Quite a few of them did, and they never wrote another good book between them. Fiesole, Taormina, the less popular parts of the south of France . . . You know the form. This one drifted to Vittorio. It's quite a type.'

'Alas.'

'Well, Adams is one of them. That's all I know of Adams.'

'Is he known to the police?'

'Possibly, but this is a tolerant city, sir. And not for throwing bombs about.'

'All right, we'll scrub Adams. The last on my list was a man called Luthman.'

George Bailey sat up. 'But that's rather more interesting. I meet him around, there's a sort of local Rotary——'

'Why are you interested?'

The stringer hesitated, choosing his words; at last he said deliberately: 'Carl Luthman is a Swede and he's been here a very long time. I know little about Swedes except that they always seem either to be on top of the world or just on the point of suicide, but normally they trot home again when once they've made their pile. And this Luthman is solidly prosperous, not *bella figura* at all.'

'*Bella figura?*'

'Face—a good show. It's the besetting Vittorian weakness, you know. If you happen to be a company you build an enormous skyscraper and if you're making money privately you buy a flashy motor car, a villa and all the rest of it. Or you hang it round your wife's fat neck.'

'I see.' Russell was enjoying George Bailey. 'Go on about Luthman. What does he do?'

'He runs an import and export agency and it's a very good

thing indeed. He exports anything that's offered but the imports are more specialized. He brings in engineering goods, components for almost anything. And he's always nipping over to the States.'

'He'd have contacts with SAGA?'

'I'd be astonished if he hadn't. He's pretty big in his line and he's been living with an ex-Monti.'

'It's remarkably little—even to make guesses on.'

'I know it is. Would you like me to poke about a bit?'

'No thank you, not yet. But don't go out of town unless you have to.'

'Understood, sir.'

They had finished their coffee and Bailey rose. Russell wished him good night, then walked to a telephone. He looked at his watch. He had forty-five minutes to catch his plane and if he bestirred himself he could still make his booking. Instead he rang and cancelled it.

He walked from the telephone, smiling. It was fair bookie's odds that there was nothing with Luthman, but there'd been a smell at that *questura* and Donnini had been too glib by far. And Russell hadn't known of Sir Duncan's heart. Sir Duncan hadn't told him that, Sir Duncan wouldn't. Old friends with hearts—Charles Russell knew what that meant. Perhaps it wasn't logical but his original obligation had increased. And Neil Stoddart couldn't handle this alone. Russell had liked him but had recognized a type. Neil might be sensible if and when the pinches came or he might simply charge bull-headed; he had an Ulster stubbornness which Russell, an Anglo-Irishman, mistrusted; he'd see things in black and white perhaps, he might even go all Protestant.

Moral judgements were fatal in practical affairs.

Charles Russell went quietly to bed. He had adequate reasons to stay in Vittorio but he hadn't really weighed them.

He hadn't tried, he liked the place.

*

Carl Luthman had spent the evening less pleasantly. Franchin had clearly failed him and he considered his own position. It wasn't so different from Angelo Franchin's for he too was under pressure.

It had begun a few months before on one of his trips to America, a meeting at a too-hearty business luncheon with an executive of Gatescraft. Gatescraft was a subsidiary of Amalgamated Aircraft, perhaps the most powerful as it was certainly the largest builder of aeroplanes in the world. Carl Luthman had found himself sitting next to a soft-spoken man from the Pacific coast with 'Gatescraft' in his buttonhole. Luthman hadn't been particularly interested since he'd come to the States to buy not sell, but his neighbour had been sociable and had asked him to lunch next day. Luthman had had appointments, but he knew that a refusal would have been taken in very bad part. It had been that sort of business luncheon and he had accepted because he must.

To his surprise he had found himself in the New York offices of Amalgamated Aircraft itself, lunching in the directors' room and with Garnett Anderson in person. The food had been terrible but the conversation interesting, for Anderson, in his cautious way, had been making a proposition. Mr Luthman, he'd said, was a man of substance in Vittorio and in Vittorio was SAGA. That gave them an interest in common.

'. . . Yes?'

Yes. It was openly known in the aircraft industries of the world that SAGA was building a medium-haul aircraft with British financial backing and British engines, and it happened to be exactly the aircraft which Gatescraft had been studying for eighteen months, one with a market which potentially was enormous. But Gatescraft had been doing rather more than study; they were in fact within distance of production, though that wasn't common knowledge yet. No sir, it was not.

Luthman had been interested but not very much. He was an importer not an industrialist.

So Mr Luthman would understand the situation. Whoever got his aircraft flying first would have a headstart which his competitors could never hope to overhaul. That was the way it went with aeroplanes. Mr Luthman would well know that.

He heard himself say: 'And so?'

So there were several things which could be done about the *Princess Rose*. To begin with she could be knocked.

Luthman hadn't been astonished. He was an importer not an industrialist, but he had plenty of contacts with the world of aeroplanes. It talked genially of ethical trading but it used every means possible to disparage a rival product. Short of buying space in the newspapers to say that the *Rose* wasn't airworthy (the advertisers wouldn't have stood for that) Amalgamated would seize every occasion to knock her, to black her, to make her seem suspect. And this as a matter of course. Its own salesmen would be schooled in it—the shrug when the *Princess Rose* was named, the question invited but never directly answered. Never. The lie direct was considered unethical and moreover it could sometimes be disproved, but the lifted eyebrow, the subject changed too suddenly . . . . Your salesmen would be taught all this and not all were precisely salesmen: some of them were specialists in this and in nothing else. And there was always the State Department. It had representatives everywhere, and all civil servants were more ambitious than they admitted. They knew which side their bread was buttered. Amalgamated had a lobby, well paid and professional.

Carl Luthman had said quietly that he'd no experience as a knock-man.

That was true perhaps but it wasn't important. He could take an opportunity if it offered but he wouldn't be expected to make them. He might, however, do other things. Garnett Anderson thought he could.

He had changed the subject smoothly. Mr Luthman had come to

America principally to lay his hands on some electronic equipment which was in very short supply. There was no secret about that since he was known to have tried everywhere, and so far without success. This particular funny-box was particularly difficult to get hold of, therefore, by definition, particularly profitable if you could. There would be a very handsome margin on re-sale in Vittorio. Now it happened that Garnett Anderson knew a seller. Immediate shipment of quite a lot.

Garnett Anderson had drunk some deplorable coffee. So that brought them back to the *Princess Rose*.

Now Luthman had listened with genuine interest. . . . So he was to take any chance that offered to add to what was already a well-organized whispering-campaign against the *Rose*, but his main function would be to *delay* her. He could do that—no one better; he had the contacts in SAGA and all he need do was use them. Money would be made available for his necessary, er, expenses. Lots of money and in cash.

Carl Luthman had gathered the strong impression that if his, er, expenses were accountable it wouldn't at all be strictly.

It had looked money for the oldest rope and this evening he was thinking it might have been. It might have been if he hadn't made one serious mistake. For Luthman was greedy as well as shrewd and the fatal combination had undone him. He had left Amalgamated and gone straight to his New York broker. He had a very good broker or thought he had, and the broker hadn't been enthusiastic about an investment in Gatescraft. It was a good enough firm, controlled by Amalgamated though not wholly owned by it, but it specialized in medium-haul aircraft which at the moment seemed unfashionable. There was supposed to be a new one coming up, a winner if it ever flew commercially, but the word round the market was that an Italian firm was six months ahead with a similar project, and there were English engines immediately available.

Luthman had told him to buy. He had bought steadily as his appetite rose, and before he'd quite realized it the greater part of his private fortune had been sunk in the shares of Gatescraft. It had looked the killing of a lifetime. It couldn't come unstuck—it couldn't.

And now it had. A fortnight ago he had received an urgent telegram from America: Mr Garnett Anderson would like to talk to him at once. He had caught the next plane.

And on arrival had telephoned Anderson. He couldn't get past his secretary. Finally his original contact in Gatescraft had rung him. Mr Garnett Anderson did not know Mr Luthman; he couldn't even remember meeting him. But a representative would be calling.

He had done so that evening, a man whom an earlier generation would have had a simple word for but who today had been promoted to the rank, style and title of operator. He was a man in his middle fifties in an expensive suit, and with a powerful Lakeside accent which Luthman suspected had been cultivated. And what he said froze Luthman in terror.

At first Luthman had feigned outrage. 'But I was to *delay* the *Princess Rose*,' he said.

'Okay. All perfectly ethical as far as it went. Nobody asked you to cut in on the profits.' A long finger waved minatorily. 'That really wasn't honest, was it? But now you have you're in it good. You'll take orders and like it. You'll have to.'

Luthman had seen it at once for he wasn't stupid: he'd overdone it and carelessly. His shares in Gatescraft were in the name of his nominees in London, a merchant bank which it would have been impossible to suspect of blowing him, but Amalgamated had fifty-one per cent of Gatescraft and no American corporation could be expected to be incurious when perhaps a quarter of the remaining forty-nine appeared to be held by a nominee bank in London. Any sensible board kept an eye on its Register, especially when it

34

answered to a man like Garnett Anderson. Luthman had heard about Garnett Anderson; he hadn't always chaired Amalgamated. He wouldn't have wasted time with the nominees. They were Cornhill and stuffy but they were utterly reliable. No, he'd have poked around the market and. . . .

That broker had talked and probably for money.

But Luthman's visitor had returned him to a present which had frightened him; he was saying quite calmly: 'So now you're going to *stop* the *Rose*. Stop her dead in her tracks. Kill her, in fact.'

'But I can't. I haven't access to the actual works. I can't go wandering——'

'Brother, that's your worry. But if I were you I'd *bend* a man. Somebody inside SAGA.'

'I have. There's been delay already and I fixed it. That was the bargain.'

'It was. Now they want something surer. Soon.'

With the last of his courage Carl Luthman asked: 'And if I don't?'

In a startlingly different voice his visitor said: 'I beg you to think. We could have you killed, in Vittorio would be as easy as in New York, or put into hospital for as long as we fancied. But that sort of ploy is a bit old-fashioned and as it happens we don't need it. Yet. You ask me why?' (Carl Luthman hadn't.) 'Because you're deeper into Gatescraft than you know.' The voice was almost compassionate now. 'If this *Princess Rose* flies first it's the end of Gatescraft. They've a plane coming up and it's *got* to be a winner. They've nothing behind it and Anderson's getting tired of them. Amalgamated holds fifty-one per cent of their equity but that's chickenfeed to Amalgamated. If they let Gatescraft go then Gatescraft is finished. You see? I've been making some more inquiries in the market and I'd say that your holding cost an average of forty-three dollars, plus maybe the premium. Amalgamated's interest in Gatescraft is a medium-haul aircraft which may succeed

35

commercially and maybe won't. If it doesn't they'll cut their losses. Leaving you with yours. Your forty-three dollars will be worth a few cents. And you can't get out by selling tomorrow. They know too much about you now and it would make them rather angry. Rather—well, what I've just called old-fashioned. That card's in the deck still if you try to play clever.'

'I see,' Luthman said.

'I'm very glad. That's that.' The visitor moved his head. That was a largish briefcase on the table. 'And by the way, we're sending you a manservant. Or you could call him a companion.'

'But I don't need a manservant.'

'We think you do.'

Carl Luthman had a vivid memory and this evening he wished he hadn't. They'd been serious, all right; they'd meant it. Old-fashioned, they said, and that was one word for it. He shivered. And now this Franchin, this incompetent wop, this broken reed had failed him.

But he hadn't another line nor time to make one. Moreover he'd had the message from New York which he'd been fearing since his return. A man was being sent to him. The sender was sure he'd prove wholly satisfactory.

. . . Damn them all, damn them.

Carl Luthman shrugged unhappily. He unlocked his safe, taking from it a parcel. He handled it carefully since he knew what it still contained. It wasn't explosives—he'd used the explosives. He took his car from the lock-up and drove to Angelo Franchin. It was fortunate both were bachelors.

Angelo Franchin was appalled to see him. He'd decided to stick and he was sticking still—just. At his office he'd passed the most miserable day of his life, answering questions from officious policemen, walking round the pressing-shop with experts on this and specialists in that, listening to Neil Stoddart babbling in his English way about instant, but instant repairs. They were a pleasant people

36

but they had no idea of time whatever. A dozen times Franchin had almost broken. . . . Run, run while you could. That boy would break at any time, indeed it was inconceivable that he hadn't by now, so the police were playing a game with him, they were the cat and he the mouse in some obscene policeman's pantomime.

He had not run, but he was at the extremity of his nervous tether when he opened the door on Luthman. For a second he didn't believe it, standing gaping. Then Luthman pushed past him. It was agreeable to be bullying instead of being bullied and Luthman said roughly: 'By God, you've made a mess of it.'

Doctor Angelo Franchin was conscious of an emotion which he welcomed. It was hate and it was steadying; he said with dangerous politeness: 'I'm sorry.'

Luthman didn't catch his tone, he was a Swede and not sensitive. 'It's too late to be sorry.'

'Yes, I suppose it is. That boy will talk if he hasn't already.'

'*What boy?*'

'The boy I bribed to plant your bomb.'

'There's nothing in the papers about a boy.'

'Of course there isn't. You've been here long enough to know there wouldn't be. Not till he'd served his purpose.'

Luthman said unbelievingly: 'You hired a boy?'

'Did you expect me to act myself?'

'Of course I did.'

'You're asking rather a lot, you really are.' Angelo had begun mildly to enjoy himself. These absurd Scandinavians. . . . 'Did you expect me to go poking about in my own works planting a bomb to sabotage them? I'd have been recognized at once.'

'You could have chosen your time, disguised yourself——'

Angelo Franchin laughed at him.

'But you hired a *boy*—not even a man.'

'You didn't give me time to find a man.' Franchin was really happy now. This clumsy Swede, this loutish bully. . . .

Carl Luthman choked, then rushed. He swung a fist but missed by feet. Franchin had stepped back, and improbably he had a knife out. He hadn't lost his spectacles.

Carl Luthman stared, incredulous.

Doctor Angelo laughed again. 'You're thinking this is typical Italian bravado, the sort of thing you Nordics like to giggle about? I'd never dare use a knife? But don't be too sure. For this isn't Italian bravado but the coldest Italian calculation. Let me see.' He rubbed his chin with his other hand but keeping his eyes on Luthman. 'I'm going to go to prison and for quite a long time. There's no death penalty in Italy so a few extra years might not matter to me.' Angelo Franchin's voice changed for a thought had struck him. 'Come to that it might help to kill you.'

'Why?' Carl Luthman hadn't meant to ask. He asked.

'Oh, use your head.' Angelo sounded irritable. Nothing was more infuriating that these slow snow-clad minds. 'When they catch me I'm going to implicate you too. I'll do it with pleasure. They may not be able to make it stick, though I wouldn't care to bet against that either. So you've come to my flat to shut my mouth and naturally I defend myself. Yes, it might help me.'

Carl Luthman said: 'You're mad.'

'Foolishnesses.' Angelo glanced at the sideboard. Luthman had left his parcel there. 'What's that?'

'It's nothing.'

'I don't believe you, I don't indeed. It's another little present for your bent Italian friend.' Franchin picked the parcel up.

'Be careful.'

'You be careful. Catch.'

Carl Luthman caught.

'Now go and fry your own foul fish. Beat it and quick. *Fila.*'

Franchin opened the door and Luthman went through it. 'Good night,' Franchin said, 'you gothic oaf.'

Carl Luthman went back to his Mercedes. There was a manservant arriving from America. . . . He looked at his watch. It was coming up for midnight and there was a night shift at SAGA. There was a perimeter fence but there was a railway siding too. After what happened yesterday security would have been tightened, but he'd lived too long in Italy to be over-impressed by even a tightened security. He'd have to get in and that wouldn't be easy, but if they happened to be shunting there'd be the ghost of a ghostie's chance.

He didn't rate his chances high but he knew he'd have to take them.

★

Charles Russell was sleeping peacefully when the noise of the fire engines woke him. They seemed to be a block away, swinging round the corner into the Viale, their sirens shrieking, banging their inappropriately gay bells. Russell had once been caught in a serious fire and it had frightened him more than battle. He rang the night porter.

'I hope we're not on fire?'

'No sir, not us.'

'Do you know where it is?'

'I've heard it's up at SAGA.'

'Is it indeed? Can you get me a taxi?'

'It's three o'clock, I'm sorry, I——'

'Please try.'

Russell dressed quickly and ran down the stairs. There wasn't a taxi but he found one in the square. The driver was asleep in it and Russell woke him sharply. To SAGA, and quick.

At three in the morning? Seven miles out?

Russell began to count out notes—five, ten and fifteen thousand. The driver said: '*Basta*' and Russell said: 'Fast.'

But Franchin beat him comfortably. He'd been woken by the telephone, a call direct from SAGA. He ran for his car but he

39

wasn't believing it. He'd told Luthman to fry his own foul fish but he'd never believed he'd dare to. This was coincidence.

No, it was not.

He drove like a madman through the empty streets, like the madman, he remembered, that intolerable Swede had called him.

That bloody, bloody, bloody Swede.

Chapter Four

Carl Luthman's plan for entering SAGA had required a good deal of luck which in the event had run his way. Charles Russell's required no luck whatever. He drove boldly past the gatekeeper, shouting the name of Vittorio's best-known newspaper. The gatekeeper waved him on unhesitatingly. He was already taking retainers from four newspapers and he didn't expect a tip as well.

The taxi drove down the main metalled artery, the glow in the night sky guiding them, past hangars and workshops still lighted for the night shift, but empty now, the night shift fire-fighting. Soon they were in an open square, the main hangar on one side, workshops forming another two, and on the fourth the offices, the original villa which Russell had deplored. There were a score of fire engines and more arriving, a tangle of hoses and what looked like a first aid post, and the incessant shouting which deluded the casual foreigner into a mistaken impression of panic. Russell looked round him. There was an un-English amount of noise but these firemen were professionals. He spotted the Commissario and walked up to him.

'Good evening, Commissario.'

'Good morning, Colonel. And what, if I may ask it, brings Colonel Charles Russell here?'

'An unseemly curiosity.'

'Not so unseemly. You know what happened?' Donnini nodded towards a uniformed man beside him. 'The *capo* tells me that there's every indication of simultaneous outbreaks in three places. There were two in the main hangar——'

'Where they keep the *Princess Rose*?'

'Yes, but she isn't touched. The first thing Mr Stoddart insisted on was an English alarm and sprinkler. There are still minor fires there but they had time to tow the *Rose* out. She's out on the tarmac the other side. It was very quick work—it had to be. But she's quite undamaged.' The Commissario smiled. 'You can go and inspect her.'

'I'll take your word for it. And the other two fires?'

'Another was the paintshop—there.' Russell followed the pointing finger. One of the workshops was flaming to heaven. There were hoses still playing on it from ladders and gantries, but their crews had retreated. The paintshop was roaring like an enormous Roman candle.

Russell said: 'She's had it.'

'But they've a chance to save the offices.'

'That was the third outbreak?'

'Yes.'

The two men looked at the florid villa. To Russell's inexpert eye it was well alight, but it was clear that the main effort was now being concentrated on it. The fire chief was giving orders into a walkie-talkie, moving up reinforcements from the paintshop already doomed. Donnini spoke to him and he answered, shrugging.

'He says there's far to much wood inside—the staircase, all the panelling, and then the roof. And yesterday's explosion broke the windows along one side. If a wind gets up and a gust gets in. . . .'

Donnini moved his hands, palms upward. 'She'll go up like a torch.'

'Three fires,' Russell said, 'three outbreaks simultaneously.'

'I know what you're thinking—I'm thinking it too. When the experts start working on the debris tomorrow——'

They had turned to go but swung on their heeels again. The roar, the sudden glare had spun them wordlessly. The villa's main floor was now a furnace. Donnini said: 'She's gone.'

The comment was unnecessary, the building was a pyre.

There was a quick stir in the men beside them. The fire chief was staring at the villa through binoculars. Donnini snatched them, pointing them at the villa's roof. 'There's a man there,' he said. He looked again. 'Mother of God, it's Doctor Franchin.'

*

Angelo Franchin had driven out to SAGA in an increasing and uncontrollable rage. . . . Setting fire to SAGA which he'd built from a light-aircraft shop, burning his child as the English burnt those guys of theirs. A succession of muddled images crossed his mind, pictures half-remembered from an illustrated travel book, frozen lakes and mountains, forests of endless pine, and chalets almost buried in an alien cheerless snow. Then arrogant modern buildings in a city by the sea, libraries and concert halls and far too much glass to a civilized taste. No sun, no sun, but plates of the grossest food on bits of bread. A raw spirit he'd smelt once.

Barbarians.

Franchin was an Italian, self-analysis wasn't a vice of his. If it had been he'd have recognized his daemon. It was the sudden Latin fury, evanescent and incalculable, something which turned the shakiest and most unreliable infantry in Europe into raging all-conquering tigers.

For as long as it lasted and sometimes it did.

He drove into SAGA and at once men were round him. He slipped them since he had work to do. The offices were burning and in a drawer of his desk was the dream of a lifetime, the *Rose*'s successor, no work-mare like that English *Rose*, no Martha careful of many things, but elegant, slim and beautiful, a real princess, an Italian queen, his daughter.

He'd have to get the plans out but he saw that it wouldn't be easy. The front of the villa was fairly alight and there were firemen working busily who'd be certain to stop him entering. He ran round to the back. He knew a door and the way inside.

If he could see it.

For an instant he waited, saying an *Ave*; then he went in. The smoke increased as he felt his way blindly to the foot of the staircase. Here there was light and flame to give it. Not too much flame —the staircase would still bear him and upstairs it hadn't caught yet. He ran up through the searching tongues and spurts and into his splendid office. Here there was smoke again and the glow from the fire below him.

. . . That staircase can't last out for long, I'll have to work quickly.

He had moved to his desk and unlocked a drawer when a sudden wind blew in on him. Instantly the room was an inferno. The panelling went up like straw and a hard wall of water poured angrily through the window. It knocked him down and he crawled to the door, then to the head of the staircase. He pulled himself upright, a hand on the carved wood finial. He hesitated, praying again.

The staircase disintegrated into a raving well of flame, from basement to attic the fire reached freely. The skylight fell in but he dodged the glass.

He ran down the corridor. He was drenched and shivering and afraid for his life, but there was a ladder to the roof, his only hope. The last part of his thinking mind was telling him that it was hopeless. The joists were wood and they'd been talking about replacing them.

The roof, the roof, away from the fire.

He staggered through a small trap door but stood appalled. What had been the dome of the staircase well was the muzzle of a remorselessly blazing gun. The roof had caught already, licks of flame which crept round his feet, went out, came back again in another place as he looked at where they had been.

He backed away to the parapet. Behind him in a corner was the watchtower, serving no proper purpose but which no villa of this time had dared neglect. It was an ornament and a vulgar one, but at the top was a flagstaff and a flag was straining strongly in the increasing wind. Let into the brickwork was a succession of iron rungs. Angelo Franchin began to climb them, away from the now flaming roof. A searchlight spotted him squarely but he saw nothing.

*

On the ground below Russell and Donnini and the fire chief were standing apart. Russell said to the last:

'Can't you get a man up to him?'

'I don't give men orders which I couldn't carry out.'

Russell was silent. This was a language he understood.

But the fire chief was speaking into the walkie-talkie still, and men were running with a safety net. They spread it and held it; waited. They shouted at Doctor Franchin.

He didn't seem to hear them. He'd climbed half-way up the tower and there he'd stuck. He didn't look down and he didn't move.

The fire chief said miserably: 'I've seen this before.' His voice changed urgently. 'That wall,' he said, 'it's going to fall.' He shouted into the radio and the men with the net jumped clear. For a second nothing happened, then the wall fell out deliberately. The tower fell on top of it. There was a crash and a burst of flame and dust. The dust settled slowly before the flame.

Mario Donnini crossed himself and Charles Russell followed. This was a Christian country.

Chapter Five

Carl Luthman had returned to his flat in the small hours with a sense that his stars were with him. He would have been irritated, and with good reason, at George Bailey's casual insult that Swedes were a people who swung between suicide and excessive optimism, but he was aware that he himself could swing. He was easily shaken and, in reaction, so resolute as to surprise himself. He had in fact just done so.

He had driven to SAGA knowing that the chances were against him, for he wasn't of an age to climb fences which he suspected were electrified at night nor to force himself past guards who in any case might be able to identify him later. His chance had lain in the single spur of railway, and if he'd been lucky he'd also played his luck. He had left his Mercedes in a copse along the highway, then walked to the level crossing in the perimeter fence. There hadn't been a train but there had been the stir which presaged one, men on the other side with lanterns, even a bell ringing in the crossing-keeper's hut. He had hidden and waited, then, as the freight slowed, swung himself on to an open flat, squeezing between its load of packing cases. There had been a bad moment on the other side when the rake had stopped and a couple of men had checked it, but it had been well after midnight and the men half asleep. Their check had been perfunctory, a ritual which they'd paced for far too long without event. When the train began to move again he jumped.

Thereafter it hadn't been difficult. He'd walked openly and with authority, a well-dressed middle-aged man whom it was nobody's business to challenge once inside. There'd been another bad moment when he'd met a patrol but he'd wished them a brave good night. They'd looked at him and returned it. He would have liked to plant in the *Rose* herself, but he saw at once that it was out of the question. Men were all over her, flies on a cake, but he had managed to drop a couple in the hangar. Two more in the paint-shop and three around the office block. That was his total of seven. It wasn't, he knew, a professional job, but he'd never been trained as a burner. Getting out had never worried him since he'd often visited SAGA. They checked you in meticulously, ringing from the gate to whomever you wanted to see. Who countersigned a stub they never looked at. He had walked out freely and had even been saluted. Just like a Roman office, he thought sardonically, or, so they'd told him, the English Queen's Treasury in London.

He drove home in the conviction of a job well done, and with a sense of self-respect regained. For he had been feeling a little ashamed of himself; he'd been threatened and it had frightened him. They could kill him, they'd said, or they could put him into hospital, and of the two he'd feared the second more. Phooey! It had been an extravagance from some *giallo*, some blood-and-guts shocker. And they'd sent him another message about the arrival of a manservant. Bluff again. Even if he did come, what could he do? Vittorio was a wide-open town, you could lose a fortune more easily than you could make one, but it was absurd to suggest that you could mug or kill a respectable foreigner with impunity. Especially when he was rather rich, especially when he paid his kick.

48

Carl Luthman had paid for years and now he smiled. Man-servants indeed—some strongarm to frighten him! On the contrary, he had a vast amount of money sunk in the shares of Gatescraft and he was entitled to protect his investment. Well, he'd just done so.

Back in his flat he had mixed a drink; he had run a hot bath and lain in it half dreaming. He felt good again—clean. People giggled at his country and he resented it. He returned to it seldom, but he'd been there the year before and what he had seen he hadn't admired. This smug little community, these prosperous classless burghers with their drinking bouts and sexual heats as predictable as a bitch's—impossible to believe that this was a country which had once been the scourge of Europe, the heirs of Wallenstein and Gustavus Adolphus. That was a private opinion which torture wouldn't have dragged from him and his hackles rose when he heard it expressed. Only a week ago in his favourite bar. . . .

Two Italians had been laughing over a newspaper. The Swedes —oh, come! They were rich no doubt, but they couldn't be taken seriously. Germany would have gobbled them if Germany had won, and the Russians would do precisely that at precisely the moment it suited them. Their army—what of it? It was something they hired to a stranger flag where its reputation for ill-discipline had been greater than anything African. When the going got tough its commanders resigned. No one even protested—the commanders just went quietly home.

Luthman had got up and left. He had considered a scene but had known it would be useless. . . . 'I'm a Swede and you've got it wrong. . . .' There would have been instant apologies. How could they know he was a Swede? He'd been talking good Italian to the barman, he didn't dress like a Swede nor look like their idea of one. There wouldn't have been a cathartic row. They weren't that kind.

Their idea of Swedes, of Sweden. Jokes about Stockholm having

49

more psychiatrists than New York, sniggers about the heavy food, witticisms, more than a little laboured, about the high standard of living and the low standard of everything else. They made him sick. He wasn't that sort of Swede at all—what's more he'd just proved it. Sending him a manservant . . .

Phooey and phooey and phooey.

He got up from his bath and made himself coffee. Then he drove to his office in the glow of a calm euphoria.

*

Mario Donnini hadn't been to bed either for he knew that an attempt at sleep was useless. He bathed and shaved and his wife brought him breakfast. Then he went to work early.

The first paper he saw was a report on a broken boy: under a resumed alternation of pressure and kindness he'd broken early that morning while Donnini had been at SAGA, and he'd been hired by Doctor Angelo Franchin to sabotage the hydraulics.

Donnini put the report aside for he saw that it didn't advance him. The boy wasn't a communist but neither was Franchin. So neither was the man behind Franchin. And there must be such a man. First it wasn't conceivable that the managing director of the aircraft division of SAGA would sabotage his own works pointlessly, and second it was at least improbable that the fire last night had been raised by Franchin himself. Donnini had met Doctor Angelo Franchin and he didn't think him capable of a coldly continuing viciousness; he might act on an impulse or under pressure from another man, but if he'd really raised the fire it seemed very unlikely that he'd also have got himself killed in it. Such facts as were known supported that he had not—Donnini had checked them already. Doctor Franchin had been woken by a telephone call from the works and had promptly gone there. No doubt that proved nothing, but once he'd arrived he hadn't behaved like a man with a guilty secret. Such a man, a managing director who was a torch in his own establishment, would have done everything to divert suspicion; he would have taken over the fire-fighting, given orders and fussed. Instead the Doctor had done the opposite. Men had met him but he'd slipped them, running straight to his office. For some papers perhaps, just conceivably for the evidence of the earlier delays which it now seemed he'd plotted. They'd probably never prove that now for Doctor Franchin was dead.

That line was cold but another was hot—too hot. Donnini was off his original horns but another pair and sharper had impaled him. He had nothing to fear from the communists now, nothing from the discovery that a cousin of his had been involved in sabotaging SAGA. For almost certainly he hadn't. No, but somebody else had and that somebody else must be Mister Big. Donnini was a policeman but he had a long experience of how politics worked. Catching the Mister Bigs was seldom healthy—this was Vittorio—and the sort of Big big enough to risk sabotage at SAGA, the enormously powerful SAGA, could be very big indeed.

He might even be a foreigner or at least be foreign-inspired.

Mario Donnini sighed. This was a situation where failure would be dangerous but success very possibly more so. He didn't want to find himself policing some hamlet in the Abruzzi. It could happen distressingly easily; it had happened to better men.

He turned from reflection to active work. . . . Slip an agent into SAGA? He had considered it after the bombing but turned it down, since it would have been to invite a liability without advantage he could be sure of. The Professor wasn't the kind of man to take kindly to police spies openly, and if he'd slipped in an agent secretly and something had gone wrong again (as indeed it had, he thought) the whole weight of SAGA, the Family, the whole formidable apparatus would promptly have made him whipping-boy. Mario Donnini could congratulate himself on at least one successful decision.

And now? Mario wasn't a man of unbending principle, but he was a conscientious policeman who'd do his duty while they let him. He had no sort of start but he did have a policeman's memory, and he'd remembered that a few weeks ago he'd heard a story about the *Princess Rose*. It had meant nothing at the time but now he telephoned for the report.

It was a strange little report, and it had been Donnini's impression that the Inspector who was making it was covering himself against some future possibility rather than offering information which he believed to be significant. He, the Inspector, had a friend of some importance (a relation of course, Donnini decided) and this friend had approached him for advice. He was a prosperous man not averse from becoming more so, and it had occurred to him that even with the new road tunnels getting a car across the Alps was a considerable chore to anyone driving for pleasure. So why not fly them over? The English thought nothing of flying their cars to France, so why shouldn't the French, the Germans too, acquire a similar habit of flying their cars into Italy? There would be money in it if the right sort of aircraft were available, not the considerable freighters which could already ferry cars between the major cities and Vittorio, but something to lift the holiday driver across the mountains, something to hop the Alps in fact. It would have to be Short-Take-off-and-Landing, able to fly from small airfields and even strips, it would have to be cheap to operate, and above all it must have the generous margin of power which third generation jets would give it, the ability to climb steeply, fast and safely. With quite minor modifications the *Princess Rose* had looked just the job. The Inspector's friend had even made an inquiry at SAGA.

And within twenty-four hours an acquaintance had got in touch with him. The *Princess Rose* was an English cull but there would be an American winner ready within months.

The Inspector's friend was a business man, not given to swallowing rumour so clearly slanted, but he had thought it sensible to use his own connections, and he had gone to his friend the Inspector. The police might have sources which the business world didn't, and if the Inspector should happen to hear anything of interest his friend would be more than grateful for a hint.

Donnini sent for the Inspector, realizing at once that he had nothing to hide. He'd given the name of his friend in his report, but he didn't know the name of the friend's acquaintance. His friend hadn't given it and it wouldn't have looked well to ask. Nor could he now—his friend would be suspicious and there was no means to force his tongue. At best he would simply lie: this would be a policeman making an inquiry which might embarrass him. But it had been mentioned in passing that the acquaintance wasn't Italian. If the Inspector had erred in not including that in his report. . . .

Donnini said he hadn't and dismissed him. He then telephoned another Inspector, giving him brisk orders. He would be interested to know if anybody had recently been calling on Doctor Franchin who wasn't also a regular caller. The inquiry needn't be pussy-footed because Doctor Franchin had lived in a block of flats which also housed a notoriously crooked lawyer. So the porter was on the *questura's* payroll already. And be quick.

A quarter of an hour later the answer came back. Doctor Franchin had had a visitor yesterday evening, a foreigner. The porter had never seen him before. He'd known the number of Franchin's flat but not how to find it. The porter had told him.

. . . Accent?

The Italian of a man who had lived in Vittorio for some time, but there *had* been an accent still. The porter knew many foreigners and he was certain it wasn't English or French. German perhaps, but he rather thought not. It hadn't been *hochdeutsch* but sort of, well, *strangled*.

Donnini thanked his Inspector and put on his hat and coat. He walked to the Stock Exchange and found his broker.

'Anything to tell me, friend?'

'Steels are on the slide again.'

'Thank you for getting me out of them.' Donnini hesitated; he would have preferred to approach delicately, feeling his way towards the final question, but his broker was a busy man. In compromise he said: 'Let's have a coffee.'

'Five minutes—no more.'

They walked to the crowded bar and both sat down. Donnini said quietly: 'I'm looking for information.'

'You have the air. But you must remember——'

'I'll remember.'

'Then come at me gently.'

'Right,' Donnini finished his coffee. 'Do you know who dealt for Doctor Franchin?'

The broker said blandly: 'A very sad business—I saw it in the papers.' He looked at Donnini. 'It was lucky he left no widow.'

'I'd have said he was fairly rich.'

'He had been rich.'

'Indeed?'

The broker said deliberately: 'I'm a stockbroker with clients. But you are the Commissario.'

'It is perfectly understood.'

'So be it. *I* broked for Franchin.'

'Successfully?'

'No. Franchin was a gambler not an investor. He hadn't normally much to play with, but a few weeks ago he started in big. He bought on the margin and lost the lot. A hundred thousand dollars.'

'*Dollars?*'

'Dollars. I can't trade in dollars, you well know that, but that's what he paid me in. Cash. I'd guess he had too much to change

54

himself.' The broker looked quickly away. 'But there are citizens in this township who'll pay over the odds for beautiful free dollars. In hundreds and in thousands. Brand new bills.'

'I see. And thank you.'

Mario Donnini went back to his office. He had the story a policeman wanted now, a springboard to jump away from.

But at whom? The Commissario considered his resources without enthusiasm, envying Charles Russell, Mario Donnini was on a political spot, but the Security Executive existed to operate in the political penumbrae, the forests and shadows which Mario feared, the jungle where friends were enemies. He'd given Charles Russell a modest come-on and now he was regretting it. The English had sunk a mountain of money in the *Princess Rose*—they wouldn't let go easily. Donnini envied Russell but he feared him too. The faintest suspicion that the police had a line which inexplicably they weren't pressing and there were very unpleasant things which Russell could do. Ambassadors, Ministers, the world of the Rome he hated—Russell would get busy there and that wouldn't be good for Donnini. And dollars, he thought—dollars of all currency.

Mario Donnini sighed again. Like many Italians he nursed the firm opinion, never uttered, that Europe was in the nutcrackers, caught between two barbarisms. To the east was something which made him shudder, to the west was something which made him blush.

He returned to Charles Russell. Clearly they'd have to talk again though the interview wouldn't be easy. His hand was on the telephone when the instrument shrilled under it. Russell would be grateful for an appointment. As soon as might be convenient.

★

Charles Russell had passed the early morning in the British Consulate General. He wasn't a man who normally spent much time in these depressingly pompous places but he had wanted to send a telegram in code. He had produced his card and a warrant he seldom used. He wanted a code book, by no means the highest, but something in which he could signal to America with at least the assurance that the message wouldn't be broken casually. There was the fuss he'd expected, the books of rules, finally a reference to the Consul-General himself. . . . No, Russell didn't wish to disturb him. He wanted a code book and that was all. He was carrying an authority which said he was entitled to it and a passport to identify himself.

Finally he got his code and, which surprised him, an offer to do the coding. He checked the coded message back, correcting two forgivable mistakes and four which were simply careless. That had been in thirty groups. He then let the message go.

FROM RUSSELL
PLEASE PASS TO GERSHOM
Reference Carl Luthman of this city where I am. Nothing known against Luthman but you recently reported a surprising contact in your territory. Grateful anything further, fresher, urgentest. Consulate General will pass.

(They won't like it of course, but they'll damned well have to.) He was looking at a decoded answer two hours later.

FROM GERSHOM
CONSULATE GENERAL VITTORIO PASS TO RUSSELL
As you would expect have nothing on Carl Luthman but his ex-English contact here is of double interest. So far as C.I.A. is concerned I would prefer to report by hand in London if you are interested but his normal commercial operations are considerable. He is mercenary strongarm for respectable top-league organizations which pay him very generously when it's anything not respectable. His price is high be-

cause nothing has ever been proved against him but he has formidable unproven record behind first-class protection. Bilingual in bad American and good English. At fifty-five is a little old (saving your presence) for operating directly but has two or three trusted agents. Reported that one of these has booked airpassage to Vittorio immediately. Am checking. Grateful reciprocal information any developments your end. Message ends, begin uncoded postscript. And what are you doing in Vittorio if I may ask?

Charles Russell lunched placidly, then took a taxi to the *questura*. It wasn't his habit to offer information without receiving it, and he said smiling but simply: 'This business at SAGA which is worrying us both—have you anything to tell me because I've something here to sell.'

The Commissario wouldn't have put it that way, but then he wasn't English. It was one technique and not a bad one. But he had already made his own decision, which had been that on balance he wouldn't suppress his morning's work. He had a healthy respect for the Security Executive and Russell's presence had increased it. He'd have to take Russell with him till their roads diverged more certainly. Then he'd play it by ear.

He told Russell succinctly what the morning had yielded.

'Very good, if I may say so, and much the expected background. This is sabotage for certain and clearly it's not the communists. Then a foreigner has been spreading rumours about the *Princess Rose*, but that's regrettably normal practice in a savagely hard-selling world. And another foreigner is known to have called on Doctor Franchin the night before the fire. It could have been the same one but we've nothing on that yet. And finally Doctor Franchin was bribed in foreign money, or if you don't think so you'll no doubt be inquiring where he stole a hundred grand.'

The Commissario smiled. 'No, I'm not doing that.'

'And no more would I.'

Donnini said politely: 'And now your contribution, please.'

Russell produced his telegram and Mario Donnini read it. He said angrily: 'So an American thug is coming to Vittorio. We'll pick him up at once.'

'You won't, you know.'

'Why not?'

'Because his master was once English, and he left behind him when he spread his wings a reputation for solid carefulness. This thug of his will arrive in perfect order. He'll be a tourist in good standing and you'll have nothing against him—unproven suspicions in another country, nothing whatever here. He'll have adequate money and a passport *in regola*.' Charles Russell shook his head. 'You won't be able to touch him unless he slips.'

Donnini said coolly: 'You forget this isn't England. And suppose he went straight to Luthman's flat.'

'Suppose he did.'

'Oh come, you're not a stranger here.'

'*Capito.*' Charles Russell rose. As he went past Donnini he heard him say: 'This Luthman's very respected, very rich.'

Russell didn't answer. An answer had occurred to him—'I'd feared you'd say that'—but that wouldn't have been sensible, or not between colleagues.

Donnini sat down, his eyelids lowered. If this line really led to Luthman it was even dicier than he'd thought it was. He'd heard of Carl Luthman—rich, foreign and, well, assimilated. It was certain he would have been kicking in.

Sooner or later somebody would be having a word with the Commissario on behalf of Carl Luthman.

*

Carl Luthman had worked well that day, things at the office had run for him. He'd had dinner with friends and won money at bridge afterwards. He went to bed contented.

He woke on a sudden start, euphoria gone, conscious that a man was standing over him. He had a gun in the night table and he reached for it. The man caught his hand with both his own, bending the wrist back, holding him helpless. Luthman said weakly, shivering again, hating himself: 'How did you get in?'

'Your lock's a very poor one.'

'Why have you come?'

'I'll tell you when I'm ready to.'

The visitor let the hand go, opening the drawer of the *comodino*, pocketing the gun. He stood silently, watching Luthman. Carl Luthman knew he was wet with sweat; he was utterly humiliated. He swallowed, said feebly: 'But what's your name?'

'You'd better call me Nobody.' The man by the bed looked contemptuously at Luthman. 'Nobody,' he said, '*Mister* Nobody to you.'

Chapter Six

By eleven o'clock that morning Mario Donnini was under the first of the pressures he had expected and had feared. It was pressure from his superiors, a demand for results and quickly. It hadn't come locally, for he was on excellent terms with what in England would have been his Watch Committee, and there were plenty of people in Vittorio who were considerably less than desolated to see SAGA, the Family and the Professor in an embarrassment. It was a vast concentration of power and as such respected, but Vittorio still remembered that it had once been a City State, and the Professor in particular had an arrogance which was resented. The Professor's own two newspapers were playing down trouble at SAGA but his rival's were within distance of openly rejoicing at his discomfiture. So that pressure hadn't come locally but from Rome. What was happening in Vittorio was a scandal, a national disgrace. It must be stopped at once, the perpetrators brought to justice.

Donnini had recognized the authentic accents of officialdom, the automatic for-the-record and pass-the-buck. But he had suppressed his inclination to bang the receiver down. There was information which Rome could give him and he had asked for it. This affair concerned the *Princess Rose* and the British were in partnership with SAGA, so had there been British complaints in Rome? There had been a moment's hesitation, then an answer he hadn't expected. As it happened there had not: the British were playing this notably cool. No young man had called at the Ministry, the sort which, posted two years in Rome, still couldn't speak Italian. That was unusual and at least it was a breathing space, but another incident at SAGA and it wouldn't be a polite young man but something of higher calibre. And that couldn't be ignored. The British might be slow to start but undeniably they were tenacious once they did, and it was the bland assumption of every Englishman that what damaged his interests in a foreign country must promptly be rectified by the foreigners concerned. If it wasn't there would be increasing pressure.

Donnini had been relieved but his voice hadn't shown it. He had said that he was doing everything possible, but if Rome had any suggestions. . . .

The voice at the other end at once went cautious. It wasn't its owner's business to advise on detail (nor, Mario thought, his habit to invite the risk of doing so) but no doubt the Commissario had done everything which suggested itself. The Commissario, of course, would have been examining the wreckage of this fire? Mario said he hadn't but that the experts most certainly were. Finding evidence of fire-raising was work for men trained to it. . . . But SAGA itself—no doubt it was now full of men of his? Mario said it wasn't and the voice promptly changed again.

. . . Why not?

It could be done without difficulty, it could be done in an hour. And when the half-dozen Deputies who were the Professor's placemen descended on the Ministry, no doubt the Commissario could rely on complete support—hullo?

There was nobody there.

Donnini put the receiver back. He was a good Vittorian, at any rate by adoption, and he shared the good Vittorian's contempt and disdain of Rome. It was the capital of the country—it was nothing. A swollen bureaucracy, a circus of foreign diplomats, government *in vacuo*. No industry except the cinema and that was in disarray. A mountain of ageing paper, priests, princes and prostitutes. And to the ancient gibe he might have added an international society which, if it wasn't the most corrupt he knew, was easily the most boring. A shell of what had once been power, a tourist town, a nothing. It lived on the taxes the northerners paid, their industry, their energy. It was high time the place was sacked again.

He turned to the top paper on his desk. He had read it already and it had cheered him. At least this was factual, something a policeman could bite on. He reflected, then rang up Russell. 'We move,' he said.

'I'm glad.'

'Arrives this American your telegram was talking about.'

'My compliments.'

'On picking him out? But it was hardly a triumph of police work. It told you I was putting a man on, and there aren't that many Americans flying direct from New York to Vittorio. The tourists of course, but you can spot those easily. Mostly they board buses and drive away. This isn't tourist Italy. The rest are on business, and we've been watching the airport since you showed me that telegram. We've had two false trails but yesterday evening we found our man.'

'You're sure you've got the right one?'

'Perfectly sure, and for the perfect reason.' Donnini waited. This was a denouement and he had all of his race's love of it. He said at last: 'Of course we were following him, and he went straight to Carl Luthman's flat.'

He'd been playing for effect and was disappointed he didn't get it. Russell said casually: 'Was Luthman expecting him?'

'Perhaps, but not at that hour. His friend opened his door with the fourth key he tried on it. My shadow saw him do it.'

'Interesting.'

The Commissario hesitated for this wasn't the reaction he'd expected. This formidable Anglo-Saxon unnerved him. Finally he said lamely: 'I find it so too.' He put down the telephone, conscious of a certain lack of courtesy.

Twenty minutes later it wasn't courtesy which was worrying him. His secretary had come in with a card and the Commissario had looked at it. Mr Frederick Adams. He told her to show him in at once for he knew about Fred Adams.

He knew about Fred Adams and very much more than Bailey had. He was an expatriate Englishman, and Donnini had seriously considered running him out of Vittorio. Two things had constrained him: first he was a man of genuine tolerance, and second and more important to a Commissario of police, Fred Adams's protector was one of the three most important men in what was still Vittorio's largest political party. Such a scandal would have broken him, but it would also have broken Donnini, and this particular political party happened to be his own. He disapproved of much about it, especially its Roman connections, since like many good Catholics he was also an anti-clerical. He much disliked trade unions which took orders from their priests. Look at the men who rose in them, men like Pasquale Massaro, frighteningly ambitious and more frighteningly unscrupulous. The whole set-up offended him, but with all its faults it was still his party and the hobbies of its leaders were private matters for the confessional. The fact remained that Fred Adams was close to one of them; he wasn't a man to be given the brush-off.

He was shown in now and sat down. He had thinning hair which Donnini could see was dyed, the long petulant face of the disappointed intellectual. He stretched elegant legs which ended in handmade shoes. The Commissario envied him his shoemaker but

63

nothing else about him. A certain complication was the breath of Mario's public life, but his private affairs he preferred to keep simple. He was contentedly married and he had a carefully-chosen *amica* in a weekend flat at Rapallo. Which, he remembered, was presently proving useful for that dangerous cousin Renato Dagrappi. It was a straightforward arrangement which all sensible Italians would approve. Donnini meant to keep it so.

He listened to Fred Adams as he made his points, emphasizing them with a cigarette-holder which Donnini thought far too long. There weren't many of them and they were made with English brevity. Adams was calling on behalf of a Mr Luthman. Carl Luthman, it seemed, had been foolish in America. The details weren't relevant since Vittorio wasn't America, but Mr Luthman had been candid about the foolishness. He had indeed telephoned from his office earlier that morning—telephoned to a friend who was also a friend of Adams's. Mr Luthman had been indiscreet in the United States, and now some gangster had arrived to blackmail him; he'd even forced his way into his flat the night before and there he was lying low. So that was the situation and clearly it wasn't tolerable. The Commissario wouldn't expect that the name of Mr Luthman's friend be mentioned—he'd have called himself if that had been desirable—but it was one which the Commissario would know, one very well respected in the party, and Adams hadn't called to conceal that there were mutual obligations between Carl Luthman and this gentleman. They were obligations of long standing and considerable extent. The Commissario would understand? He did? Then that was perfect.

Mr Frederick Adams had glided off, and the Commissario considered over two very strong cups of coffee. He was fairly in the pincers now, the one side Roman, the other local, and of the two he feared the local more. A fuss from Rome was one thing, a distant bombastic voice demanding action, a voice which had cut the line when asked for backing. But this visit from Adams had been much more immediate. It didn't disturb Donnini that he was evidently expected to relieve Carl Luthman of an unwelcome visitor: on the contrary he had already considered it, for he was a conscientious policeman when allowed to be and the affair had put his back up. Sending some thug into his manor as though Vittorio were a colony. . . .

It was a personal insult and Donnini was a Sicilian.

That aspect would be easy or at least it would be possible, but there was another much more dangerous. He'd spent yesterday morning in solid routine police work about the sabotage at SAGA, and what had emerged had been a line towards some foreigner. That foreigner could be Luthman though the evidence wasn't complete yet nor Donnini's mind quite made up on it. But Russell's might be and that could be disastrous. The head of the Security Executive would be indifferent to telephone calls from Rome, even more so to local politics; he would be interested in SAGA, that the *Princess Rose* should fly on schedule. If he was thinking of further sabotage he'd work on it remorselessly. The first piece of positive evidence that Carl Luthman was involved and Russell would come running to Donnini. If he didn't get action he'd go flying off to Rome himself, and not to some official in a Ministry.

Whereas Carl Luthman had protection, really excellent protection.

Mario Donnini permitted himself another coffee, though he was already beyond his ration for the morning. Somehow Charles Russell must be diverted from Carl Luthman. Nor was that aim quite hopeless. There wasn't a shred of formal proof, and in any case Russell wouldn't be interested in bringing saboteurs to court for past offences. If he thought, as Donnini did, that sabotage had shot its bolt, that any further trouble must be different, then it wouldn't be quite unprecedented to help a colleague in a difficulty. So the position must be explained to him, that Luthman was hot, too hot for the Commissario.

But how? Tell him in words? The Commissario shook his head. That wasn't the Italian way and it was his instinct it wasn't the English. No, he'd have to be *shown*. Russell might be undemonstrative, a thought too laconic for an honest Italian taste, but it was certain he wasn't stupid. He would take a hint, above all a hint in action.

Mario Donnini telephoned to him. 'I was a little abrupt just now,' he said. He spoke in apology.

'So am I when I'm busy.'

'Have you pressing engagements?'

'None I can't break for you.'

'We were thinking of paying a visit to Luthman's flat. If you'd care to come along with us——'

'I certainly should.'

'You know there's some sort of American there who interests us both. We've still got a man on him and he hasn't left the flat. Mr Luthman went to his office this morning normally, but he usually returns about six o'clock. I see advantages in calling when both are there together.'

'I think I follow.'

'You do?' Mario Domini doubted it. 'I think you're at the admirable Manin?'

'I am.'

'Then may we call for you at half-past six?'

'I'll be ready,' Charles Russell said.

*

Nobody—Mister Nobody to Carl Luthman—had had instructions to temporize. Two attempts at sabotage had failed, and a man called the boss was a very angry tycoon indeed. He'd had considerable hopes of sabotage and had still not quite abandoned them. That was one reason Nobody was being sent to Vittorio—this

Luthman might still be useful. The other was that he knew too much. So no violence for the moment, the moment meaning simply till it was certain Carl Luthman was useless. Nobody was to await instructions and to make his presence felt. For the moment no nonsense. Further orders would reach him.

It was an assignment he hadn't fancied and by that evening he was already bored. He had raised no objection to Luthman going to his office; he had to get some sleep himself, and in any case he couldn't have prevented it short of the violence they'd prohibited. He had slept and shaved, then settled with a cigar. He never drank when working. He knew a little Italian, enough to read the news-papers, and what they had told him had set him wondering about Carl Luthman. Early that morning he'd been a middle-aged Swede, obscenely frightened, but the fire-raising at SAGA could hardly have been done by this Doctor Franchin who'd died in it. It could have been this frightened Swede—he'd ask him outright this evening—and if it had been Carl Luthman it was an action of some courage. So, in its way, had been getting the breakfast. Luthman had lain in bed an hour, apparently a broken wreck, then silently had got up and dressed. He had gone into the kitchen and Nobody had smelt coffee. The clock flying eastwards had wrecked his digestion with meals he hadn't expected, and he was prepared to pay for coffee, even to help to make it.

But Luthman had waved him aside. He had shaved with a steady hand, his shoes were clean. . . . No, he could manage perfectly. And did *Mister* Nobody—the faintest ironic emphasis—did Mister Nobody like eggs with his breakfast?

He had said that he did and now he sat wondering. He spent a good deal of time on racecourses, and his word for Carl Luthman was in-and-out runner. He wouldn't have risked a dime on him. Of course he was a Swede, and everyone in the underworld knew that Swedes were unreliable. Just the same it was interesting. You broke into this Luthman's flat and he lay in his bed and sweated.

And a few hours before it was possible that he'd been personally sabotaging an aircraft plant which had already once been sabotaged. It didn't make sense but then Swedes didn't. They went up and they went down again, and when they were up the sky seemed the limit.

Nobody smoked quietly till Luthman returned at six. Carl Luthman took his coat off and changed his shoes. Returning to the living room he said: 'Would you like a drink?'

'I never drink on duty.'

'Very wise.'

Mr Nobody reflected. 'Will you tell me something, please?'

Carl Luthman smiled. 'I expect you could make me.'

'Then did you raise that SAGA fire—yourself, I mean?'

'Why don't you use your tiny mind.'

Mr Nobody stared at him. This Swede was up, he was indeed. Nobody mistrusted it.

*

Mario Donnini was punctual at the Manin and Russell climbed into the police car beside him. The Commissario was driving, and there were two armed and uniformed *carabinieri* in the back seat. Russell settled happily for he believed he had read the signals. He was going to be taught a lesson, a polite little lesson that Vittorio wasn't England. The Commissario had remarked the fact already. They were going to arrest a foreigner and Russell wondered curiously what technique they'd adopt to do it. . . . His passport? But hardly. It must have been in order for the man to have entered at all. That he'd used a key on Luthman's lock? That was a possibility but it wasn't a matter which Russell himself would have leaned on very heavily. Nothing had been forced. Then some question about his registering with the police? That again was a possibility, since he wasn't staying at a hotel which would fix it

68

for him. He had seven clear days to do it, but it looked the best of several bets. The regulations would be Italian, complicated and contradictory, and something could always be found in them.

Charles Russell's private money was on some bureaucratic fiddle.

They drew up outside Luthman's block and the four men went up in the lift. The *brigadiere* rang the bell and Luthman opened. The uniformed police gave creditable salutes and Donnini introduced himself. He did not introduce Charles Russell. 'I think we've met before,' he said.

'Of course. I remember perfectly. And where.' Luthman didn't say where.

'I believe you've a foreign guest and I must trouble him with some questions.' Donnini waved a hand. 'The merest formalities —you know how fussy my masters are.'

Luthman swung the door wide and all of them went in. The flat was beautifully furnished. Nobody was in a chair still. He rose in a compact movement, waiting. Russell could see that he'd noticed the policemen's pistols. Luthman said pleasantly: 'These are policemen, as you can see. The shorter of the two in plain clothes is very senior indeed.'

Mr Nobody didn't answer and Mario Donnini spoke; he said officially: 'We have reason to believe that you're carrying a firearm.'

Charles Russell blinked but he didn't speak. He knew what was going to happen.

This certainly wasn't England.

'No, I am not,' Mr Nobody said.

'I must beg you to be careful in what you say. If you've brought an unauthorized weapon into this country it could be very serious.'

'I know that. I haven't.'

Charles Russell was looking at Nobody. He was sure he was telling the truth.

Carl Luthman had slipped away but now returned. 'I think you should come this way,' he said. He was playing a part and playing it well. He was the law-abiding citizen, regretful but always dutiful.

They went into the spare bedroom, Luthman first. One of the *carabinieri* had his hand on his holster but he hadn't yet drawn. A drawer of the dressing-table was open and an automatic lay on a pile of handkerchiefs.

Luthman said simply: 'I knew he had it.'

He had known indeed, since it was the pistol which Nobody had taken from him. He had bought it in America where the purchase had been cheaper and above all a great deal simpler. He'd never fired it in his life but he'd felt happier to possess it. In Vittorio one never knew.

There was silence while the policemen took Nobody away. He went past Carl Luthman with a very odd look. These Swedes, he was thinking, and when they were up . . .

The Commissario put gloves on, wrapping the pistol in the largest of the silk handkerchiefs; he put it in his pocket and wished Luthman good evening. Charles Russell bowed. He hadn't spoken but he'd been watching Carl Luthman. He was an experienced judge of men and he had recognized a type. His opinion of Luthman wouldn't have been different from Mr Nobody's. This man could be dangerous. All manics were.

Russell and the Commissario went down to the street again. The *carabinieri* had taken the police car but another had arrived. It all struck Charles Russell as admirably organized. They climbed into the second car and Mario drove away. Russell said softly: 'You once told me this wasn't England.'

Mario Donnini began to laugh. 'You think it was all a plant?'

'Of course.'

'As it happened it wasn't.'

'Oh come. You started talking about a pistol, a pistol appears——'

'A gun was *going* to appear.'

'I'm not sure I follow.'

Mario Donnini had stopped the car and now he wasn't laughing; he felt in his other pocket, coming up with a second pistol. 'That one,' he said, 'but I fear without fingerprints. Carl Luthman thinks fast. You have to in Vittorio.' Donnini had started the car again. 'You learn to think quickly and other things too.'

'I find it easy to believe you.'

'I'm glad. Because some of the other things could be interesting to the Executive.'

'Ah yes?' Russell said.

'For instance that you can't make a fortune in Vittorio without also making powerful friends.'

'Friends in the police?'

'No, I didn't say that—that takes it too far.'

'I didn't intend offensiveness. Let's say friends whom the police hold highly.'

'That puts it more fairly.'

Russell said thoughtfully: 'I can recognize a warning.'

'A warning! My very dear Colonel——'

'I like a man who chooses his words. Would hints suit you better?'

'Perfect.'

Russell began to laugh in turn. 'It would be deplorable if a respectable British official were discovered carrying firearms. Or maybe his passport isn't quite what it should be.'

'Colonel Russell, I beg you! Come to my office. We will drink to our understanding.'

'The Manin is much nearer.'

In the comfortable bar Russell ordered a Krug he knew and approved. He had a sense of the occasion and clearly this was one of them. They settled to the magnum, and forty minutes later walked together to Mario's car. It had collected a ticket which the

71

Commissario tore up crossly. 'These stupid city police,' he said. He wasn't quite tight but he wasn't quite sober.

'The man on the beat—God bless him.'

'I beg your pardon?'

'Nothing—an English proverb.' Russell opened the door of the Commissario's car, and as Donnini started the engine said: 'I can recognize a hint, you know.'

'You said so before.'

'I know I did. And I like a man who can choose his words.'

'You said that too.'

'One gets repetitive with advancing years.' Charles Russell's voice changed suddenly; he shut the door with a firm clean snap. 'I said I could recognize hints,' he said, 'I don't undertake to accept them.'

Chapter Seven

Unlike Mario Donnini Charles Russell had been under no pressure, chiefly because he had a long experience and a painfully acquired skill in foreseeing and forestalling it. He had been telephoning daily to Sir Duncan Stoddart, aware that he was one of the few men alive who could restrain that formidable old man from immediate and what might well be disastrous action. Russell indeed had been behind the fact that no formal complaints had been made in Rome. No, he had said, that wouldn't be wise, or certainly not for the moment. Nothing was more fatal than putting the official machine in gear when it had nothing specific to bite on. It could no doubt be done, Stoddarts weren't nobodies, but the reluctant creakings would be audible in Trastevere, and if later there was something to go on, some specific piece of evidence to bang on the table, then going off at half-cock would have prejudiced proper action. On the other hand it was a good idea to send somebody down who understood security. SAGA would stick its toes in against an influx of police agents—this was Italy, in particular it was Vittorio—but two or three quiet Englishmen from one of two organizations which Sir Duncan would have heard of. . . . It was already in hand? Excellent. But no, it wouldn't be sensible to come rushing down oneself. Very far from it.

Sir Duncan had grumbled. If he'd been only a few years younger and his doctors less exigent . . . and the whispering campaign, the smear-the-*Rose* had started again full blast. What did Russell make of that? He made little and said so. It could support an opinion that further sabotage was unlikely but it was far from conclusive that other mischief wasn't brewing. As to that it was guesswork. This was a situation which must be allowed to simmer gently. Vittorio wasn't Belfast.

Sir Duncan had asked an old and respected friend about his son. How was Neil Stoddart facing his first big crisis? Charles Russell had thought well enough. The *Princess Rose* wasn't damaged, and though the loss of records and offices would be serious, Neil had moved in caravans and was working a twenty-hour day. The paintshop had been expendable. Russell hadn't seen him again, he hadn't indeed expected to, but Neil had telephoned with a dour incisiveness which his father would have approved. Neil Stoddart would do.

He would do, Russell thought, just so long as he kept his place. That was putting it bluntly but it wasn't unfair to him. His place was his father's representative, a junior director in his first major job. But he was short on experience, the type who would see things in black and white, and if he saw himself as a principal, even worse as a trouble-shooter, the results might be embarrassing to those whose professional business was discreetly shooting trouble.

Russell's reflections were interrupted by the arrival of their object. Mario Donnini had said that the experts would discover something but in fact it had been Neil. He put on Russell's dressing-table a tube of some plastic perhaps a foot long. 'Will you take a look at that,' he said. It hadn't been a question: he spoke as formidably as his father.

'If you'll tell me what it is.'

'It's a modern incendiary. It should have burnt itself out and left

74

no trace, and it would have if it had been handled properly. Instead I found it when they dug out Angelo.'

'Unfortunate Doctor Franchin. You want to talk about him?'

'No.'

'I think you're wise since he's now irrelevant.' Russell nodded at the tube. 'A dud?' he asked.

'Not quite. The charge is all right—thermite and something else, I think. And to fuse it you turn the top. Like this. Every click is ten minutes.'

Russell said: 'Carefully.'

'It's quite all right, I've taken the charge out. But I found the thing set at zero.'

'What do you think happened?'

'Who knows? Maybe whoever planted it panicked—the others went up together, synchronized. Or maybe he dropped it and the fuse bounced back to nothing.'

'You've been handling it without gloves, I see.'

'I know—I didn't think.'

'I don't suppose it matters. Whoever planted it would have known enough to be wearing them. But the Commissario's going to be cross with you.'

'You want me to take this to him?'

'Certainly.'

Stoddart said bitterly: 'The police haven't helped us much. Delays to the Rose which we're now sure were organized, then a bombing and now this fire——'

'They haven't had much to go on yet. Listen. Take that incendiary straight to the Commissario. Admit that you brought it first to me but tell him expressly that I sent you along with it. I've a certain relationship with Mario Donnini, and naturally it's delicate. I'm a foreign official in a very foreign town. If I put a foot wrong I'm finished, perfectly rightly, and sitting on factual evidence would be as improper as it could be. In any case, what could I do with it?'

'I take the point, sir.' Neil Stoddart spoke with reluctance but he picked up the incendiary. It was evident that he was a little disappointed in Colonel Charles Russell.

'And come back here and lunch with me.'

'I'm really rather busy, sir.'

'And so am I.'

Neil Stoddart looked at Russell. He didn't look busy but Neil could recognize an order. 'Thank you, I'd like to. At one o'clock?'

'At one.'

Russell waited an hour then telephoned to Donnini. Donnini was polite, so polite as to give the impression that he had written out a brief and now was reading from it. He thanked Colonel Russell for his valued co-operation; he used the word several times. Correctitude wasn't mentioned but Donnini made it clear that Russell's conduct had been correct; he valued that too in a relationship which without it could decline into mutual embarrassment. Russell, in fact, was Donnini's favourite foreigner. The Commissario said largely that he would co-operate in turn—on any occasion, at any time. He gave Charles Russell his private telephone number and Russell wrote it down.

He was about to hang up when Donnini began again. 'The experts are working on that incendiary,' he said.

'It looked American-made to me.'

'Possibly. I just thought you might like to know that it certainly isn't Swedish.'

Donnini rang off.

Charles Russell smiled, settling in the bar to wait for Stoddart. It was a lunch he'd been looking forward to, since Stoddart's character was an important thread in the tangle which lay before him, indeed in certain circumstances it might even be decisive. Russell was too observant not to have noticed that he got on exceptionally well with younger men, but he had never analysed the flair because he never played it consciously. In fact the gift had a simple spring: he seldom thought of men as younger except to reflect that at a similar age he'd had different but much less tolerable defects. He had no cronies at his club, only a private list of bores he fled, and he wasn't at heart conformist. He was a pillar of the establishment but its values were quite alien. It could make him laugh sardonically lest otherwise he weep, and it could often make him angry. He knew that the young felt a shadow they feared and hated and that they reasonably blamed their elders for a life which might end tomorrow. Charles Russell seldom apportioned blame but his own view wasn't dissimilar. It was his private conviction that Europe as he understood the word had committed suicide when he himself had been nine years old. Everything that had followed had been merely the obsequies, the best one could hope for that they be conducted with decorum.

They went to their table and Stoddart ate fast—too fast. Russell could see that he had been working too hard, that the responsibilities of a first big job which was going wrong had tensed and strained him. He might be ready to talk and Russell would let him.

Over brandy he did so and Russell listened. To Neil Stoddart the situation was predictably clear, predictably because he himself was predictable. Everything that had happened at SAGA had been a communist plot, right down to bribing Angelo Franchin if he hadn't been secretly a communist. Admittedly there was another aircraft industry with a powerful interest in destroying the *Rose*'s prospects, but if they'd had a hand in it, all right they were using the communists. It was the simplest assumption and therefore the best.

Russell opened his mouth but shut it. Listening to other opinions was invariably more profitable than antagonizing their owners by pointing out tiresome objections. Russell kept silent and Neil Stoddart went on. So clearly it was the communists and Neil

Stoddart meant to stop it. Moreover he believed he could or at least that he had a chance of it.

Charles Russell asked politely how.

'I mean to try to buy them off.'

'But whom will you buy?'

'I've been lucky in that.' Stoddart spoke modestly but with decision undiminished. 'I know an important communist, I met him playing golf. He calls himself Dagrappi though I dare say that's not his name. I'd played with him quite a bit before somebody told me he was a communist big shot. We were pretty friendly by then and I asked him outright. He didn't deny it. He'd been sent up here, from Rome I think, and he's either Number One or Number Two. Not the shopwindow One or Two—the real one. That's how they work.'

'I know.' Charles Russell reflected. 'So you mean to buy Dagrappi off?'

'I know what you're thinking—he'll take my money and go on as before.' Neil Stoddart shrugged. 'I can't deny that could very well happen, but at least I can cut the risk. I thought of offering him a retainer, the rest to be paid when the *Rose* flies on schedule.'

'I can see you're your father's son.' Russell ordered more Vecchia Romagna, to his taste the least damaging of the destructive local brandies. 'When do you mean to meet him?'

'Tomorrow's Sunday and I'll motor to Rapallo.'

'Your friend's not in town?'

'He isn't. He rang me a few days ago and suggested a game down there. The course is a joke but it's the prettiest in Italy. He was perfectly frank again. He was sent here from Rome but the police have got on to him. Not enough for a formal rap, it seems, but sufficient to squeeze him out for a bit, to get him away from Vittorio.' Neil Stoddart looked at Russell. 'That would be normal form, you know.'

'I believe you, I do indeed.' Russell spoke with conviction. This was Mario Donnini in action again and probably in person. The thought gave him pleasure—so he wan't the only man Donnini had tried to hamstring. He marked him up more mental points, then asked what seemed a necessary question: 'If Dagrappi's in Rapallo not Vittorio——?'

'How could he control things here? I think he could. They may all be scoundrels but they're remarkably well disciplined.'

'There,' Russell said, 'there I can agree with you.'

'But not about buying Dagrappi off?'

'I haven't said that yet.'

'Of course if you've a better plan——'

'I haven't. I wish I had.'

'Then I'll leave early tomorrow to beat the Sunday traffic. Six-thirty, I thought. I'll go to bed early and with luck I'll get some needed sleep. If I start at six-thirty——'

'Ye-es.'

'I beg your pardon?'

'I'm afraid I was wandering.' They had finished their brandy and Russell rose, walking with Neil Stoddart to his car. It was a red Aston Martin and Russell admired it generously.

'A present from Father,' Neil Stoddart said; he swung on Charles Russell with a hint of desperation. 'If I let the old man down——'

'You won't.'

Russell walked away slowly. 'If I let my father down,' he thought, if he let down Sir Duncan . . .

This decisive, unsubtle, wholly admirable young man. Russell genuinely liked him, he really oughtn't to risk his life. It was perfectly normal practice to bait the hook, but when the bait was the son of a very old friend . . .

If he didn't accept his chances he'd be nowhere. Donnini had tried to hobble him, he'd been here a week though it seemed much less, and already there'd been rumblings from London about returning. The pros were this and the cons were that, or perhaps the fish would ignore the bait.

Russell's hunch was that he'd take it. That was one of the most dangerous stretches of road in Italy.

Charles Russell went back to his room and thought. He had never accepted that Luthman could be working solely for masters who paid him. The hypothesis didn't cover the facts, or it had to be stretched implausibly. Here was a Swede in his later forties, prosperous and even rich, and with legitimate connections in America. Where there was an aircraft industry with a self-evident interest in destroying the *Princess Rose*, people already fighting her with a wicked campaign of smear. They could easily have gone further—it wouldn't be the first time. So Luthman lived in Vittorio, SAGA had its plant there, and it was perfectly acceptable that the parties had come together. But it wasn't at all acceptable that sensible Americans would hire a middle-aged trader and assign him in person to sabotage. No, Luthman had been the fixer.

Had been—now he might be much more. The motive could only be money, not some fee as an agent but an interest as a principal. Shares in the company which was trying to kill the *Rose*, a percentage when her rival flew. . . . Charles Russell shrugged. The details weren't important but the principle was essential. If Luthman was in this personally Russell had to be sure of it, surer than the moral certainty that Luthman himself had raised the fire at SAGA. And Donnini was protecting him—that stalemate must be broken too. Two birds with one stone.

A dangerous, an uncertain stone, a David's pebble.

Charles Russell undressed and slept an hour. He had a simple faith in what more complicated men called unconscious cerebration; he called the same thing sleeping on it. When he woke he had decided, reaching for the telephone unhesitatingly. He rang George Bailey.

Bailey was to present himself at once.

80

Chapter Eight

Carl Luthman had an engagement that Saturday evening and was wishing that he had not. He would have liked a quiet evening to consider his future quietly, but he had an invitation from an important customer and his absence would be noticed. His mood was one he recognized, a momentary balance between a legitimate sense of triumph that he'd neatly got rid of Nobody and the growing realization that he'd lost a potential ally. His only effective ally. If only Amalgamated hadn't been quite so brash, if only they hadn't thought solely in terms of duress. Recollected in satisfaction, in the knowledge that this thug was off his back, it didn't seem unreasonable that Garnett Anderson should have sent someone to keep an eye on him. After all they had an object in common and Luthman had taken Amalgamated's money—quite a lot of it still, even after wasting some on that broken fool Franchin. Somebody who could have helped him wouldn't have been unwelcome. Instead they'd sent a hatchet man and Luthman had had to get rid of him. They'd presented an ally with what in effect was an ultimatum and that wasn't good diplomacy.

Carl Luthman laughed. He'd had a postcard from Mr Nobody, though he didn't suppose it had been written voluntarily, and it had been posted at a frontier. That, on the contrary, had been diplomacy at its Latin best. There were at least two charges which they could have brought against Mr Nobody, but Nobody was an American. His consul's duty, his training and personal instinct, would have been to defend him as far as his arm would reach, and if that wasn't far enough to invoke one which did. If Nobody had been English, now, they'd probably have jailed him. British consuls weren't American, the English held them in scant respect. They'd do not what they could but what they must. They had plenty of books and they'd fly to them automatically; they'd find you legal aid no doubt, and if they were exceptional you had a modest hope of not being clobbered in custody. Then you'd go before a local court and the consul to another post. Quite possibly on promotion. He'd have done his job as his masters saw it.

So Nobody had been pushed across a frontier and it was certain he wouldn't get back again. Carl Luthman was conscious that in a real sense he was missing him. It was unlikely that Garnett Anderson would communicate with him directly, even more unlikely that he'd dispatch another bully, but action was still necessary and Luthman saw no way to it.

He frowned unhappily, his mood changing sharply. Action was still necessary because more than half of his private fortune was sunk in the shares of Gatescraft. Wall Street was bearing them strongly, the ex-Englishman who had first called on him had been an alarmingly accurate prophet. If the *Rose* flew first then Gatescraft wouldn't be worth much, and if Amalgamated cut its losses then Gatescraft would be finished.

So would Carl Luthman.

He saw that he had two hours to kill and he put on his coat and began to walk. Charles Russell had walked to watch the people, but Luthman unconsciously walked for reassurance. He went down to the business quarter. It was Saturday evening but men were still working. The shops were open, the shoppers milled purposefully, and there were lights in the business skyscrapers and banks. There were whey-faced men in the cafés of the Galleria, arguing vociferously and always on the make. This wasn't the Italy of the tourist office brochure, the broken peeling churches and the improbably blue sea. Even the Duomo had a pleasantly brisk vulgarity. Vittorio—what a city! Luthman had learned to love it. Even as a boy he'd felt stifled in Sweden, but here an individualist could thrive as an individual. No wonder that these Vittorians should dislike and despise their capital. *This* was the capital, *this* was where the work was done which meant where the money was made. Plenty would disagree with that, plenty would talk of a new social order. Carl Luthman didn't agree with them, he'd never demanded security.

Nor, he reflected, had it. In twenty-five years in this roaring town he'd known very bad times, once almost bankrupted before his wits had really sharpened, hanging on with a loan at an exorbitant rate of interest. He hadn't resented that he had been brought to this by sharp practice, nor had he borne malice when at last he had fought his way back. He still did business with the man who had almost broken him but he did it now much more carefully. He walked past the Opera, shouldering off the ticket touts. The First Citizen had a one-night stand but he wasn't an admirer; he thought she could act but mistrusted her voice. There was a creak in it now, the resin of advancing age. She was good enough for London still but hardly for Vittorio. Let her bring down Covent Garden then, they wouldn't know the difference.

He went into the Galleria by the northern entrance, finding an empty table, ordering the Barolo he always drank. Beside him two men were arguing furiously about a proposition which it was clear that neither believed in. Talking cost nothing, and somewhere in this chaff of words was perhaps the seed of a new idea. For an instant Luthman loved them. He loved the gestures, the fire which he knew to be half affected, the sheer un-Nordic rattle and show.

Or the lawyer behind them matter-of-factly explaining to a client that he'd been fortunate: the judge in that particular court could hardly cost more than two hundred pounds.

Yes, a fine city, but not to be poor in, not to have to start again. Luthman wouldn't be quite penniless if Gatescraft crashed, but it wasn't the point of Vittorio to be a man of modest means there. You were rich or you were nothing; you accepted the standards, you couldn't simply dodge them. Carl Luthman had lived in Vittorio since his arrival as a stranger and now he was more Vittorian than the Vittorians. He had no intention of going back to Sweden on what would still have been a competence: on the contrary his appetite had grown. He had mapped the future clearly —the business turned into a company, himself as chairman, the villa at Menaggio whence he'd motor in three times weekly, the controlled decline into a respected but still potent old age.

That wasn't a future to give up easily. Damn Garnett Anderson, damn Amalgamated. They had an object in common but they weren't being helpful to him. Very well then, he'd fight for his own. There was a cliché about protecting one's investments. When it came to the pinch, though, it wasn't a cliché.

He rose from the table, leaving a carefully calculated tip. It wasn't a mean tip but nor was it generous; it was the tip of a man who used that café often, a man of position who asked and received the service which was appropriate.

He began to walk home briskly in the increasing cold. It was all very well to decide to fight alone. But how? Luthman shrugged in his fur-collared overcoat. Further sabotage was impossible— SAGA by now would be crawling with every sort of security man, and in any case he had exhausted the tools of violence. No bombs, no incendiaries, no means to restock them even if he had thought it sensible. But there were surely other methods and he began to consider them. Financial pressure? That existed in principle, it was even conceivable that Amalgamated might exploit it, but Luthman was too realistic to suppose that he himself could bring any sort of pressure to bear on SAGA. The Family could swallow him like an olive at one of their cocktail parties. No, he needed something practical, something he could handle here himself.

He found himself thinking again of Nobody. He'd read a library of paperbacks about crime in America and most of them had left him with the sour taste of scepticism. Nevertheless some astonishing crime took place with apparent impunity, beatings and muggings, kidnappings and hold-ups, men who came to threaten you by night. And all of it beautifully organized. There was a precedent for everything and Nobody might have helped him. There was Neil Stoddart, for instance—there were possibilities in Neil Stoddart. He was the only son of an old, sick father. To kill him would be pointless and to kidnap him far too risky, but the fact remained that he was a pistol at an old man's heart. Sir Duncan could be reached that way more surely than through his pocket. He was tough but old, a sick man too, and Neil was an only son. If he thought Neil was threatened, that perhaps there'd be a second time, somewhere, someday, but this time deadly serious . . .

He wouldn't think first of the *Princess Rose*.

Luthman frowned irritably. This was copybook theory but it was useless to Carl Luthman. Shoot at Stoddart and miss? Have him beaten up judiciously? Absurd. It was theory—forget it.

He went back to his flat and changed his clothes. He didn't expect to enjoy his evening but at least there'd be plenty of alcohol. They were promoting this four-wheel drive saloon, the Press would be there and the foreign buyers, and Luthman knew what that meant. There'd be whisky unlimited and he intended to use his share of it. Action in theory—he was sick and tired of theory. Whisky was fact and tonight it would cost him nothing.

★

When George Bailey arrived at the Manin he was evidently excited. Russell recognized the symptoms. No stringer worth his salt who did not secretly nurse the hope that one day he'd be entrusted with a job beyond keeping his ears open and reporting to the Executive. The more impressionable indulged romantic fantasies—pistols and knives and safe-blowings. Russell knew that one of them had even started to learn judo at something the wrong side of fifty. George Bailey was a Yorkshireman, too practical for fantasy, but he arrived very quickly, and metaphorically with his tongue out. Russell gave him a drink and began on a gentle questioning.

'I think you once told me you'd met Carl Luthman?'

'Yes sir, I've met him around. There's a sort of local Rotary——'

'I suppose it doesn't meet tonight?'

'No, not on Saturdays.'

'Could you somehow manage to meet him this evening? I mean without its looking contrived.'

George Bailey considered, then asked to use the telephone. He rang his office, speaking English, then hung up and returned to Russell; he said in a rush: 'One of the big car people is throwing a promotion party this evening for a new model, and one of Luthman's import lines is components for motorcars. It's a very fair bet he'll be there and I've a friend who could take me too.'

'Good.' If Russell was pleased he was showing it only slightly. 'Now listen. Do you play golf? Does Luthman?'

'I do, Luthman doesn't. But he belongs to the country club. He more or less has to.' George Bailey laughed. 'Golf's that sort of game in Vittorio.'

'Then there's your lead-in. Get hold of Luthman and start talking about golf. Bring it round to who's good at it. That clearly includes Neil Stoddart. Mention him by name. You know him, I take it?'

'Yes, sir.'

'Then spill it out casually that Stoddart is going to Rapallo

86

tomorrow and you presume he'll get a round in on that charming little course. Go on about how he'll eat it up, but keep golf as the theme and Stoddart as the variations. You follow?'

'I follow so far.'

'Then switch to how you'd play more often at Rapallo yourself if the traffic wasn't so frightening at week-ends. Neil Stoddart beats that one by starting very early. Six-thirty on the dot and it's a habit.' Charles Russell poured more whisky. 'Now please repeat that back to me.'

George Bailey did so, adding in disappointment he didn't hide: 'It doesn't sound very difficult.'

'I heartily disagree with you. I'd have said that if you can put that over smoothly and naturally you'd have the makings of an actor. It's the naturally which is important, which is why I'm not going to tell you why I want the thing done at all. And there's something more to come, you know. I want you to watch how Luthman takes it. He may not react, but if he shows the least sign of interest I'd be more than half-way home to where I'm groping. The *least* sign of interest. Ring me up in either case as early as you can. And if this goes as I hope it will I certainly won't forget it.' Russell smiled paternally. 'I'm sorry if you were hoping for something criminal. Some other time perhaps. For the moment, good hunting.'

Russell ate unhurriedly, then went to his room. It was ten before Bailey called him and again he was excited. 'He bit,' he said. 'He bit like a feeding salmon.'

'A very pretty simile. Now tell me what happened.'

'He made it very easy to drop your fly. He may not play golf but he does like to talk about it. He watches the tournaments and knows most of the form. In fact he mentioned Stoddart first. So I switched to Rapallo—how Stoddart took a driver at only three holes there. The rest followed naturally. Then things started to happen.'

87

'What things?'

'Well, I'd say he'd had a drink or two—not drunk, you know, but fairly high. He had a stiffish whisky in his hand when I went up to him, but the moment I dropped the six-thirty bit he put it down at once. I saw him look at his watch. Then he made an excuse about having to talk to the wife of the host and slipped me. I never saw him again, but I did one thing you hadn't told me. I found out that he spoke to nobody. He went straight to his car and drove off.'

'How do you know?'

'It was nine forty-one when he looked at his watch—I know because I looked at my own when he left me. And it was a quarter to ten when a Mercedes convertible slipped out of the car park. The party was in full swing still, and the attendant noticed because it was the first car to leave.'

'You've done very well. Where are you now?'

'Still at the party, sir.'

'Take a couple of drinks, you've earned them.'

Charles Russell sat down with mixed emotions. The first was that of any gambler who had backed a longshotter and seen it come home. He had been reasonably sure that Luthman would attempt no further sabotage but a good deal less than certain that he'd accept the proffered gambit of direct action against Neil Stoddart. An experienced professional would have seen an opportunity, have weighed and probably taken it, especially if he'd lacked another plan. But Luthman wasn't a professional criminal. That was true, Russell thought, but he'd met Carl Luthman. The meeting had been short, but for a man who knew men sufficient. This unstable type was dangerous. It was far from ideal as the agent of others, impossible to discipline, given to thinking personally. Personally . . .

There'd been some beautiful things in that beautiful flat, a Klee, Etruscan vases.

How the rich fought for it!

And it seemed that Carl Luthman was running to form. As, for that matter, was Mario Donnini. Russell mustn't offend him, the risk wasn't sensible. Instead they must co-operate—Mario himself had used the word. Charles Russell laughed aloud. Cast your bread on the waters and it was a mistake to assume that invariably it returned to you. But sometimes it did and richly. Donnini believed he had him fixed so he'd have to fix Donnini. This would do it very prettily and besides he needed Mario. Russell was sixty and wasn't armed, but one minimized one's working risks, particularly risks to an old friend's son, particularly in Vittorio.

What a wonderful, wicked, wide-open town.

Russell picked up the telephone, ringing the private number Donnini had given him. A woman's voice answered, and Russell said in his serviceable Italian: 'May I please speak with the Signor Commissario? I call myself Russell and I'm from London.'

There was a considerable delay and in the background disputing voices. Charles Russell waited patiently, for this wasn't the first time he'd heard a policeman's wife protesting at business calls to what she had once dared to hope would be a home. Finally Donnini came on the line. 'Good evening,' he said. His voice was polite but not forthcoming.

'I must begin with an apology. But you gave me your private number.'

'Yes, I remember.'

'A kind promise of help——'

'I remember that too. If I can be of service——'

'I'd like to borrow a motor car.'

If Donnini was astonished he concealed it. 'But of course. I'll send a car and a competent driver.'

'I was hoping you'd come yourself. You gave me an interesting evening once and I was hoping I could return it.' Charles Russell waited. Donnini could decline to move and from his own point of view quite reasonably. All policemen were curious but perhaps not that curious. Donnini broke the silence, smoothly humouring this eccentric.

'And where do you propose to go?'

'Rapallo.'

'*Rapallo!*' There was a very different silence and Russell listened to it intently. He couldn't see the Commissario but he knew that he'd shaken him. Not why but he'd play his luck. He said again: 'Rapallo.'

'To what address in Rapallo?' Now the voice wasn't smooth but alert and wary.

'I don't know that yet.'

Donnini said slowly, talking for time to think: 'You want me to take you personally to Rapallo?'

'If it wouldn't be too much trouble.' Charles Russell was puzzled but he could tell he had drawn an ace. Which one didn't matter yet. A single word, the name of a seaside town, had changed the Commissario from bored banter to apprehension. He was saying now deliberately: 'At what time should I call for you?'

'I'm afraid it's inconvenient.'

'Never mind that.'

'Then at a quarter past six tomorrow morning.'

'I'll be there.' For a moment Donnini recovered himself. 'And what sort of car would the Executive prefer?'

'A fast one, please.'

Donnini rang off and sat down a little shakily. The devil, he was thinking—the cunning old devil. So he'd found out about Renato and now he was fighting back with it. Donnini could see what that meant: he was between this English devil and his own infested sea, on one side Carl Luthman and the protection he had bought himself, on the other this Englishman who'd ask for immediate action against him.

And could break him in twenty minutes if he didn't play ball with him.

Donnini telephoned to the *questura*, ordering a police car without markings or insignia; he went back into the sitting-room. His wife saw his face and at once began to natter, but he silenced her irritably. He had an early appointment and was going straight to bed. She'd married a policeman and this was a policeman's life. A car would be calling for him at six o'clock next morning. This wasn't the first time and it wouldn't be the last.

Mario Donnini had gone quietly to bed and Russell had followed him. He rang down to the porter, arranging a call for a quarter to six. He had an alarm but did not set it. He'd stayed at the Manin before and was quite prepared to trust it.

Carl Luthman chanced nothing. He drove to an all-night garage and checked his tyres; he filled the Mercedes' voracious tank, then he left the splendid car outside his flat. He set his alarm for half-past five, testing it twice though he knew it worked perfectly. But he didn't expect to sleep or even try. He took fifteen grains of aspirin, then he lay down and chain-smoked.

Chapter Nine

Mario Donnini arrived at the Manin punctually at a quarter past six but he had very nearly not come. The situation was sickeningly clear to him: Russell had discovered that he had an important communist as cousin and was driving him to Rapallo to rub his nose in the mess. Why he should choose six-fifteen in the morning to do so was less clear but did not invalidate the major premise. The journey itself was entirely unnecessary if Russell already knew the relationship, and Mario Donnini had no taste for humiliation. He had nearly not come but a certain pride had brought him. After all, he thought grimly, he'd taken Charles Russell to Luthman's flat; he'd *shown* him. He couldn't reasonably grumble if Russell used the same technique. If he broke his engagement Russell would think him cowardly, and it wasn't wise to let eminent Englishmen think you were a wop poltroon. This was fair enough in its English way, and Donnini had determined that he'd behave with an equal elegance. On the parallel occasion Charles Russell had bought a magnum and Donnini had decided that he'd take Russell to lunch on this one. He'd take him to the *Excelsior* and he'd order the best of everything. It would cost a good deal of money, his lunches would be small for weeks, but if that was the English gesture he'd have to match it. Donnini was a Sicilian—scanty lunches would be a hardship but a loss of face unthinkable.

So Donnini drove up and Charles Russell climbed in. It was six-fifteen precisely. They drove through the almost empty streets, down to the southern motorway. Russell began to explain and Donnini listened. Russell was talking succinctly, pulling no punches but rubbing no salt in. He said blandly that this was Italy, that he was out of his jurisdiction and in Mario Donnini's manor. That was why he'd invited him to accompany him on what might well be an interesting morning. For Charles Russell had information. Firstly that Neil Stoddart was motoring down to Rapallo and secondly that Carl Luthman would be following him. Luthman had made that decision at a party the previous evening, and he had made it very suddenly. His motive was uncertain still but Russell had made a guess at it. That guess might be wrong, and in any case the Commissario was free to make another. But if this were all coincidence it was really rather a long one. Russell would never forgive himself if some misfortune occurred to Stoddart and Donnini would never forgive him if it happened without his knowledge. So Russell had asked him to come along too. That was all for the moment. *Res ipsa loquiter*, or would do very shortly.

Donnini heard this in silence. His first thought had been automatic: Russell was lying, he did know about Renato, and this story was some elaborate plan to add to the final discomfiture. But on reflection that wouldn't stand up. Men like Charles Russell didn't act without motive, and to lie seemed completely pointless. Last night it might have been necessary, something to get a policeman to come at all, but he had jumped to the conclusion that Russell had discovered about Renato, and here he was this morning, punctual and obedient, driving Russell to Rapallo. This story was true then, the implication excellent. Russell knew nothing of Renato Dagrappi. So. That was good.

Not so good, he thought immediately. Russell might not have discovered that Renato was his cousin, but if this story were true then it wasn't by definition some stupid bluff. Russell *had* discovered something, but something about Carl Luthman. He was sufficiently confident to have brought Donnini with him and the motives for that could be distressingly more than one. If Russell expected violence then a Commissario would be an ally, but his relationship with Russell could hardly be called alliance. He had in fact tried to warn him off, and Russell had given notice that that position was unacceptable. So this was his way of fighting back, not quite the one the Commissario had assumed, but in its way just as dangerous to him personally. If Neil Stoddart suffered mischief and Donnini were present, if Russell knew that he'd been present because he'd fixed it to be there himself, then Russell could dictate his own sweet terms. There could be no more covering-up on Luthman. That the Swede had protection would mean nothing to Charles Russell then; he'd have turned the tables deftly and he'd exploit the new position. Against Luthman of course, but alas against Donnini too. He'd have the Commissario in the open and could ask for co-operation. Donnini smiled sourly, for it would be rather a different use of a much used word. Satisfaction was much more accurate. And if Russell didn't get it he'd go flying off to those Roman pigs.

No, this wasn't so good, it might even be as awkward. This Englishman was a wide one, he might almost have been Sicilian.

They had driven to the motorway and Donnini paid the toll for a private car. As they went through the gate he said: 'Will you tell me what you're expecting, please? An indiscretion by Carl Luthman——?'

'I'm expecting to find a Mercedes convertible waiting in one of the first two lay-bys. Don't look at the driver but go on to the following pull-in. Draw into it. Wait.'

'You seem pretty sure.'

'I'm policeman-sure—you know what that means.'

They drove along the motorway, past the first of the well-spaced lay-bys. It was empty. 'When's the next?' Russell asked.

'About thirty kilometres.'

Russell looked at his watch. 'We're early still—they'll hardly be ahead of us. Keep moving but not too fast.' He settled to watch the road ahead, said suddenly, sharply: 'Don't turn your head. Drive on.'

Mario Donnini did so. He wasn't very happy but in a sense he was content. He could recognize authority and was accustomed to obey it. The Colonel Charles Russell of the Security Executive . . .

He was a devil in human form no doubt, but he was a pleasure to do business with. He was saying now calmly: 'Pull into the next lay-by, please.'

Donnini pulled in and stopped. 'And now?' he asked.

'Now we watch for a red Aston Martin.' Russell pulled a paper out, consulting neatly written figures. Say a quarter of an hour from Neil's flat to the start of the motorway—that would have brought him there at a quarter to seven. Then fifty miles on in perhaps forty minutes. They'd taken longer themselves but this wasn't an Aston Martin. That would bring the Aston past them at twenty-five minutes past seven. Russell looked at his watch. They'd started fifteen minutes earlier and it was seven-twenty exactly. He took off his watch, putting it on his knee. Twenty-one, twenty-two, twenty-three . . .

There was a blow of angry air and a scarlet flash, a full-throated engine diminuendo.

Donnini said: 'Saints in heaven.' He put a hand on the gear lever.

'Wait.' Russell was looking at his watch again, the second-hand now.

The Mercedes went past them a blurred green streak.

'Forty seconds behind,' Charles Russell said.

'For all I'm concerned it might be forty minutes. I can't live with those two.'

'We must,' Russell said.

*

Lying on his bed, smoking his head off, Carl Luthman had had time to think. He had taken a snap decision and he had taken it with perhaps a third of a bottle of whisky in his bloodstream. But now, cold sober, it didn't seem a stupid one. In terms of pressure against Sir Duncan an accident to his son, one clearly suspect of not being accidental, would open the board up and maybe more. Put at the lowest they'd have a situation of manoeuvre. Luthman was too sober to put it higher or more precisely, but he tried for the second time to think as Sir Duncan might. So there'd been delays to the *Rose*, a bombing and then a fire—these were serious matters and Sir Duncan would take them seriously. Then a threat to his son, a mishap which looked deliberate . . .

People who could contrive such things weren't fooling.

And Luthman hadn't so many cards left that he could refuse the chance to draw one. For the first time that evening he smiled. Sir Duncan apart he had private motive. He'd driven semi-professionally as a younger man, in rallies and minor races, and now in his forties he still drove well. He had a magnificent car and so had Neil Stoddart. He'd never been introduced to him but he'd seen him at SAGA often; he'd seen an Aston Martin too. It was a personal challenge and with weapons he understood. That had been decisive.

Luthman slipped from his lay-by as the Aston went past him. He knew what he'd do and had planned where to do it. Not here, not yet. Up to Seravalle it was a fine modern motorway, flat as the plain it traversed—dual carriageways. At the pace Neil was setting no driver alive could hope to contrive an accident short of suicide and murder, but once in the pass the road became a death trap in three lanes. There were double white lines, mostly favouring uphill traffic. But this was Italy. The oil came up from Genoa in convoys of trailered lorries. They were grossly underpowered uphill and downhill their brakes were suspect. The week-end traffic drove with desperate competition, and though it wasn't the rush hour yet the road was by no means empty. The stretch in the pass was patrolled day and night by tough traffic policemen who would stop a rogue car by ditching it, but Luthman had seldom driven these miles without seeing a wreck of some sort. Nor had anyone else.

He watched the red car in front of him but didn't try to pass it. He had chosen his spot and it wasn't just yet.

*

Charles Russell sat next to Donnini, sweating. The needle flickered around the ninety but Donnini was bursting her guts out. On the clock the Fiat would reach ninety-five but it wasn't the sort of ninety Russell fancied. She needed two or three miles to make it, and on any sort of curve she wouldn't hold. Then the agonizing build-up to top speed again, the absolute maximum on the next stretch of straight. The brakes, Russell knew, had begun to fade. He was frightened and not ashamed of it. They'd lost the Mercedes twelve minutes before. Without turning his head Donnini said: 'We'll be a long way behind but it isn't that which worries me. On this sort of road and at this sort of speed any accident would be genuine.'

Colonel Charles Russell thought so too. In this flat-out saloon they were taking appalling chances. He did not speak.

'But once they get past Seravalle . . . climbing curves, three-lane traffic . . .' Donnini went silent as the next bend came up at them. He made it with a squeal of brakes, the scream of tortured rubber. When they were round he spoke again. 'Get on the walkie-talkie

97

—it's there in the dashboard locker. Turn the left hand dial to zero, press the switch on the right. That puts you on the traffic net.'

Russell took the radio out, doing as he'd been told to. There was an amiable babble of morning pleasantries. The traffic, it seemed, was very light, the real work to come still. Presently a new voice came in.

'Sergeant?'

'What goes?'

'A couple of clowns at a ton or more.'

'Racing?'

'I shouldn't think so. Plenty of room between them.'

'What sort of cars?'

'Some sort of English sports car and an F.I. Mercedes.'

'They sound safe enough to me.' The sergeant wasn't an English cop, it didn't offend him that fast safe cars should be driving fast and safely. 'Let 'em go,' he said briefly.

Donnini said urgently: 'Tell them to follow them up the pass. Press the button with a C on it. Listen, then . . . Christ!'

He had lost concentration for a fatal second. It was a right-hand bend and he wasn't going to make it. He braked and the back wheels broke on him. There was nothing behind but they caught the inside safety rail. For a second the Fiat tottered, then it somehow bounced off upright. Russell had dropped the radio as he'd been thrown sideways against his safety strap. It had smashed against the door, then down. He picked it up and pressed button C. . . . Nothing. He changed to Receive and listened. Nothing again. Donnini was driving on. Russell replaced the radio in the dashboard locker. Donnini said grimly: 'Broken?'

'She's very dead.'

*

Neil Stoddart, like Luthman, enjoyed driving fast. Not that he was pushing her—a hundred was barely cruising—and he hadn't been

98

worried by the Mercedes behind him. He was a considerate driver and twice he had slowed: if he was holding the Mercedes back he was happy that she should pass him. But twice she had slowed in turn. That hadn't struck Neil as in any way curious. Plenty of people found a hundred quite fast enough, plenty were content to tag what in practice would be a pilot. The Mercedes wasn't too close to him and he knew that her brakes were excellent. Still, sooner or later she'd probably overtake him since once in the pass Neil Stoddart would be a slowcoach. The road frankly frightened him and he drove it like a funeral. He'd been passed by a Seicento there and even by a lorry.

He let the Aston lose speed and began to climb steadily, seldom over forty and in the tunnels much less. He'd seen more crashes in these tunnels than he had any wish to think about, the chain effects of too sudden braking till it came to the car with defective brakes. Somehow there always was one and there followed a concertina. Neil Stoddart drove on quietly, alert, reading this scarifying road, for the first time thinking seriously of the convertible behind him. The Mercedes was much closer now but so was the pace much less. Neil could see in his mirror that the driver wore dark glasses below a well pulled down soft hat, and that the registration was Vittorian. But this wasn't Vittorian driving form. It was one thing to use an Aston as a convenient pilot at something around the hundred, quite another to stick behind it when it was crawling like a lorry. No, this wasn't Vittorian form at all.

At the next stretch of straight Neil Stoddart dropped down to thirty. The double white line was with them and two or three cars went by with an air of aggrieved release. The Mercedes wasn't one of them.

Neil Stoddart was puzzled, he hated the inexplicable. This wasn't a country where drivers waved futile hands to please the police, but the next chance of passing and he'd try with a hand signal.

A mile later he did so but the Mercedes stayed behind him.

Neil Stoddart was uneasy now. A Mercedes was tailing him and he couldn't think why. Without being conscious of it he began to drive faster.

When it came it surprised him. The Merc suddenly flashed him and he drew in. It was a gentle left-hand curve this time and again the white lines were with them. To the right was a drop, perhaps six feet, down into an orchard. There had once been a safety rail but somebody had smashed it. Now there were warning notices. Beyond the orchard the ground swung up again to a gate and a little farm. Beyond the farmhouse was a wall of solid rock.

The Mercedes drew level and Stoddart slowed. The Merc slowed with him. Neil couldn't understand it. He knew this road well, and beyond the rock wall the double white lines changed abruptly against them. At this sort of speed the Merc would be caught in the open. It seemed pointless . . .

It was not! The Merc was trying to push him off, the driver was trying to ditch him. Neil was conscious of a taut set face, a face which didn't look at him. He was watching the hands and not the face—the right hand was moving down on him. The two cars inched nearer and instinctively Neil Stoddart swerved. . . . The orchard, a six foot drop. He set his teeth. Two could play at this game—bluff. He was already in second and he gave the accelerator a tiny flick. Then he put his left hand firmly down. There was the shocking scream of outraged metal. Neil was level with the Merc again, going slightly the faster and better placed. But another inch over and he'd be bound to catch a hubcap, or flinch to the right and there was still that broken safety rail. Neil Stoddart swore softly but he kept his left hand grimly down. For a second the cars ground appallingly on, tearing metal protesting, the naked wills of men as brutally locked. Then the Merc broke away. The driver changed quickly, skidding as he accelerated, his right rear wheel catching Neil's front left. It threw him off course but now he was past the orchard. He took the gate of the farmhouse, the top bar rearing, smashing the windscreen. For the first time he flinched. There was a tree but he didn't see it, then a crash and the noise of escaping steam. People at once came running.

Chapter Ten

A quarter of an hour later Russell and Donnini found them talking to Neil. He was mildly shaken but quite unharmed, for he'd been braking strongly and his safety belt had saved him from a head through the broken windscreen. Russell began on a brisk precise questioning and Neil Stoddart answered quickly. Yes, almost certainly someone had tried to wreck him, but no, he didn't know who. The car had been a Mercedes and the number plate Vittorian, but he hadn't recognized the driver. He'd been wearing dark glasses and a hat well pulled down, but it had been Neil's impression that he would have recognized him if he'd known him. That was all he could tell them, so if they happened to be going that way perhaps they'd give him passage towards Rapallo. He still had time for a round of golf and he could telephone to Vittorio for the recovery of the Aston. It would never be quite the same again but it wasn't a total write-off.

At the mention of golf the Commissario stiffened. He knew that Neil had met Renato Dagrappi golfing and there was therefore the possibility that he'd been driving to Rapallo to play golf with him again. That question could be asked outright but it wouldn't be wise to do so. Donnini had been thinking fast, and the last thing he

wanted was to appear before his cousin in the company of Neil
Stoddart and Colonel Russell. He couldn't prevent either of them
telling Dagrappi what had happened, and if Renato saw an advantage in that he couldn't prevent him using it. But he could avoid a
situation in which Renato might simply create one. Appear with
Colonel Russell of the Security Executive and it was frighteningly
far from certain that Dagrappi wouldn't exploit it. . . . 'My very
dear cousin Mario, whose flat this is though the name on the door
is different . . .' The Commissario mentally shuddered. Charles
Russell didn't know that yet, though Donnini had started off with
him on the premature assumption that he did. Well, the saints had
withheld the knowledge and it was a fool who fought his own kind
saints. Donnini smiled dourly. Colonel Russell would soon be
calling on him, and after this morning's incident he'd make pretty
stiff terms. If he found out about Renato too it wouldn't be terms
but complete capitulation. Mario said smoothly: 'You intend to
play golf still? Then I suggest you take my car. I ought to make
formal inquiries here, and I'll stop the next traffic patrol and radio
for a pick-up home.'

'That's really very kind of you.' Neil Stoddart turned to Russell.
'We could hire you a set of clubs, sir.'

'If I won't be in the experts' way.'

'In that case you won't be back till late.' Donnini reflected. 'I'll
send a man to the golf club to collect the car and to drive you both
back.' He put on 'both' a carefully calculated emphasis, looking in
turn at Russell. 'I think that might be wise,' he said, 'in the somewhat unusual circumstances.'

'I think that might be very wise.'

'Then it's all understood.' The Commissario knew it wasn't but
at least it was worth a sighting shot.

Russell said quietly: 'I'll bring the car to your flat since
your office will be shut today. We ought to have a word or
two.'

'But of course—I'll look forward to it.' Donnini spoke bravely but quite without truth. The morning might have been more embarrassing for him—just; the fact remained that it had still been embarrassment. His next talk with Charles Russell was something he loathed the thought of.

He watched Russell and Neil Stoddart drive away in his car and Charles Russell watched Stoddart closely. He showed none of the symptoms of shock, the garrulity, the wild statement: on the contrary the incident had sobered him, and Russell seized an opening into a mind which he saw had opened. For the first time he told him all he knew, the story at SAGA as he himself saw it, suppressing only the reason why Donnini had been driving with him. That would have been unnecessary since he'd now won his private duel with him; it might even have smacked of boasting. . . . So this hadn't been the communists but something at least as powerful. Not, Russell had said, that there was any objection to playing golf with a senior communist, indeed there could even be circumstances where the connection might be useful. But it was pointless to offer him money to stop doing what he hadn't been. So they would play two pleasant rounds of golf. Russell mightn't much like Dagrappi but he was quite prepared to respect him, and in any case it was no part of his philosophy to make enemies on principle. Neil Stoddart had listened, finally nodding. His opinion of Charles Russell had clearly risen, and he said clumsily but with sincerity that he was grateful.

He'd be even more grateful if Russell would handle his father. They'd have to tell him what had happened lest he hear from another source, and if Neil rang himself Sir Duncan might do anything. Whereas a call from an old and respected friend. . . . Russell had said he would do it gladly. Tomorrow, that is. Today they'd play golf and enjoy their lunch. They'd tell the truth to Dagrappi but not more of it than they needed to. They needn't, for instance, mention Mario Donnini. There was nothing to gain by doing so, and to a policeman there might be something unknown to lose. That was clear?

Clear enough.

They had played their threesome in an agreeable winter sun, the Ligurian sun which the travel agents boosted and which as often as not obliged them. Charles Russell had enjoyed himself. He never played golf except to win and he'd won a good match with Stoddart. Dagrappi he hadn't betted with. He was an unashamedly fierce competitor but easy money didn't tempt him.

They had walked from the comfortable clubhouse well content. The Fiat had a driver now but he wasn't in police uniform. He drove them to Vittorio, dropping Neil at his flat, and at Mario's Russell dismissed him. He'd be talking some time and could telephone for a taxi.

Donnini received him politely but in fear, though in the event apprehension had gone well beyond the fact. Russell wasn't a bully and his terms had been reasonable, limited to the objects which he had decided he must achieve. Leaving the Commissario's at midnight Russell himself considered them with satisfaction, ticking the points off mentally. . . . The contracting parties hereunto agree and bind themselves:

1. *That Colonel Charles Russell of the Security Executive shall take no action against the Commissario Mario Donnini arising from the aforesaid Colonel's knowledge that violence was attempted against Neil Stoddart by Carl Luthman, whom the Commissario was protecting or was being obliged to protect by persons unnamable.*

Charles Russell smiled, reflecting that if that was a concession it was one which he'd found easy to concede. He wasn't without sympathy for a policeman under pressures which had nothing to do with police work, since something parallel but dissimilar was part of his daily life. It was true that nobody had ever asked him to protect a common criminal but he had papers on several hundred people, some of them Members of Parliament, whom he knew to be traitors in every sense but the formally legal. He couldn't bring these men and women into court but he could readily prove their connections. Yet if he went with these files to Number Ten he'd find himself leaving quickly, and not to return to the Security Executive. Whereas so long as he remained at it there were things which he could do. Most discreetly he did them and many were illegal. Who was he to break a policeman, and in any case what would he gain by it? They'd send another Commissario whom he wouldn't even know, the same pressures could be brought on him and Russell would then be weaponless. Better the devil he knew. And there was something else though he hadn't expressed it. He liked this particular devil.

Charles Russell returned to his Heads of Agreement:

2. *The Commissario Mario Donnini shall put a twenty-four hour watch on Neil Stoddart, assuming personal responsibility for his future safety.*

That had been simple since of mutual advantage but the final clause less easy. In the end it had been a compromise:

3. *The Commissario Mario Donnini shall further put a twenty-four hour watch on Carl Luthman, sharing with Colonel Russell any developments of interest. 'Watch' shall be interpreted in this context as all such action as will not be noticed by Luthman and therefore complained of to the further embarrassment of the Commissario.*

There had been some tough but good-tempered bargaining on this item. Charles Russell had wanted the works—a tap on Luthman's telephone and the means to record any conversation in his flat.

But these Donnini had stoutly fought, insisting that they were too dangerous. Too many people must necessarily know of them, and if Luthman could substantiate that the police were really after him he'd go running to his protector again with a complaint which the police couldn't duck. These suggestions if pressed would be at variance with Clause One, since they risked action against the Commissario—local action which, SAGA and Colonel Russell quite apart. Donnini feared more than the displeasure of some mandarin in Rome. Russell had argued but had finally agreed. Donnini's case had been persuasive and Russell had left it that he would leave the details of surveillance to the police. But he reserved his position (he'd used the cliché distastefully) and if anything happened which he considered should not he would feel himself free to take such action as best suited him. That meant suited him personally, and Donnini would have to take it if the present position broke down.

They had shaken hands formally. Not a word had gone in writing and Russell certainly hadn't suggested it. He had a string on Donnini and as long as he could twitch it he was happy. That was better than any document. Russell wasn't a civil servant, far less a lawyer.

In his taxi back to the Manin he reflected on a fruitful day. He paid the taximan generously and went quickly to his room. On the way he left instructions that he wasn't to be called—he intended to sleep late and would ring when he needed coffee. The exercise had relaxed him, the situation had gently clarified. One complication had been eliminated, Mario Donnini now saw more or less eye to eye with him, and Russell's instinct and experience were to eliminate complications. Of course Luthman had been neutralized rather than defeated unconditionally, but unconditional surrender was a doctrine which Russell mistrusted. Look what happened to Europe when inexperienced transatlantics got the dogma up their noses. But a good day, a useful one . . .

Colonel Charles Russell was fast asleep.

*

Renato Dagrappi too thought his day had been well spent. Here was the head of the Executive in Rapallo, and Donnini had already admitted that Russell was interested in what was happening at SAGA. Naturally. He had his job, as Donnini had, though they might not be quite the same. But why had he come to Rapallo? Not to play golf; he wasn't dressed to play golf and he hadn't brought his clubs with him. Renato dropped casual questions and the answers were as casual. Neil Stoddart had had an accident and Colonel Russell had been behind him. Odd. The same road, the same hour. An early one. And in a car which Renato suspected. He'd never seen it before, it hadn't 'Police' above the number plate, but it was the model which senior policemen mostly used. It could even be Mario Donnini's.

Renato Dagrappi had hidden a smile. He had realized at once that this couldn't be all the story but he saw equally quickly that for himself it was enough. The fact that a story existed was enough. He'd been exiled from Vittorio in a game of squeeze and counter-squeeze and he'd been waiting till the balance broke, till the beam tilted back in his favour. . . . Some foolish excess by a sergeant of *carabinieri*, some municipal contract which Donnini was taking his cut on. . . . This affair wasn't either but it would serve him just as well. These two amiable Englishmen had something to conceal: one of them was embarrassed, quite possibly both. Russell and Donnini had an object in common, so if Russell was embarrassed then probably so was Mario. That was sufficient for the moment—he'd soon nose out the details in Vittorio once he was back there. His cousin was a Sicilian like himself. Both men knew the rules and neither would think of breaking them.

Renato waited till Russell and Stoddart went, then he packed his few clothes quickly; he bumbled back to Vittorio in his ancient Seicento; he went home.

His home for three months had been a two-roomed flat in one of the stark blocks which Russell had preferred to a decaying English suburbia. It was sparsely furnished but not quite uncomfortable, its only unusual features an expensive modern wall safe and two telephones. Renato Dagrappi began to use them at once. He had known that the line at Rapallo would be tapped but he had very good reason to be sure that these were not. His organization was particularly strong in the postal services. He was very out of touch and began to change it. As he telephoned steadily his lean face hardened. After perhaps an hour he stopped.

His face was very serious for so was the situation.

*

Carl Luthman had driven on to Genoa, then turned right and right again, slipping back to Vittorio through the Giovi pass, then the old road by Alessandria and Mortara. He'd never met Stoddart face to face and he was reasonably sure he wouldn't recognize him again, but he could recognize the car, especially with half one side off. Well, it had been an accident, there'd been nobody there to say it wasn't, but that, if it came to it, was still in the future. What was immediate was to get himself back to Vittorio, and it would be stupid to risk the motorway with the scars of a serious collision. The traffic police wouldn't arrest him merely for driving a damaged car, but any damaged car was suspect, particularly at week-ends, and they might stop him and ask questions—where, when and how? They'd take his name and particulars, then they'd start to make inquiries, and as Neil could have complained to them they'd link the two promptly. They might do that in any case since one couldn't hide a damaged Merc indefinitely, but it would take a good deal longer if he didn't complete the equation for them by getting himself booked for some suspected but unknown accident. And what he needed was time, every day of it possible. For time was running out on him.

Luthman garaged the Mercedes and locked the door carefully; he lay down on his bed but he did not relax. He was more exhausted than he had ever been but he was far too tensed to sleep. The day had scraped him raw and wincing. Failure, he thought, and failure doubly. He'd failed in his aim and the failure had been avoidable. It had been a personal challenge and with weapons he understood. And Neil Stoddart had defeated him. In the seconds when their wills had clashed it had been his own left hand which had come weakly down, it was he who had broken contact. He remembered the two Italians who'd been laughing in a bar. They'd be laughing again if they knew what had happened. And this time rightly—that made it unbearable. These Swedes were all the wringing same.

Luthman writhed in a humiliation which racked him physically; he groaned but did not hear himself. And his weapons were being blunted one by one. He still had a card, one which he might already have played if Garnett Anderson hadn't rushed him into sabotage. But you couldn't invoke sabotage without paying a certain price for it, and part of that price was alerting the people sabotaged. A man might be venal, outrageously ambitious too, but he might not do now what would once have seemed a working risk. Not even for money, a great deal of money.

Carl Luthman sighed. Money was money—he hated to risk it. But he rose from his bed for he hadn't an option; he was in this inescapably. He went to the telephone, dialling a man he knew.

Pasquale Massaro said that it would be difficult now. Double money. . . ? That was interesting certainly, but money wasn't the present obstacle. There had arrived an English Colonel from the Security Executive and the Executive was much more dangerous than the *questura*. But eliminate this Colonel and by all means they could talk again.

Yes, Luthman had heard him correctly. Perfectly correctly. He'd said eliminate and meant it.

Chapter Eleven

Charles Russell woke late next morning and stretched contentedly. The exercise had done him good, he had slept like a child for a solid nine hours, and he was feeling the gentle glow of a well-preserved maturity. And just as well he should be, he reflected over coffee, for it would be premature to assume that he now controlled the table. A little local difficulty had been adjusted, Donnini would play normal ball so long as he didn't lean on him, but it would be a mistake to suppose that because violence had been tried and failed therefore the game was over. That wasn't the modern pattern and in the Executive patterns were vital. Its head drank his coffee quietly but he knew very well there was a long road ahead still. He was living in times when violence was almost normal. Once it had been a last resort, perhaps because of a different ethic, perhaps because men had lacked the tools. Charles Russell shrugged. In the Security Executive moral judgements were irrelevant and he himself made them rarely and with distaste. What mattered practically was that his enemies would have cards still. He couldn't even guess at them —if he could he wouldn't be waiting for the other side to move.

So he'd wait a little longer since he'd have to. The prospect didn't distress him. It was his seventh day in Vittorio but the rumblings from London that he return at once had ceased. They had ceased with a Safehand letter from the Minister he answered to. Certain rumours had been reaching him, matters about the *Princess Rose*, and the Minister had been delighted that Colonel Russell was already in Vittorio. Charles Russell might further take it that it wasn't only a single Minister who was pleased to hear of his presence there. The government wasn't behind the *Rose*, or not in the sense of direct investment, but she might earn much foreign currency if she were really what Stoddart's believed she was, and that wasn't something to be lightly tossed away. Indeed it was not. And if only a half of these rumours were true what was happening was an outrage. No government could tolerate that a supposedly friendly country. . . .

The pompous phrases had ground on and on, but Charles Russell laughed. For his original hunch had been right—this wasn't the first time a private chore had flared into public politics. He had telephoned to the Executive, arranging for a courier. Anything of importance was to be flown down to him daily, when he'd deal with it and fly it back. There were four flights a day. Two of them were English, the food accordingly, but on the others a man ate well.

Russell rose and bathed, enjoying it. His courier would arrive about eleven and it had occurred to him to send Sir Duncan Stoddart a letter by his hand. But he had turned the idea down. Nothing was more alarming than a letter by hand, and when the words spelled violence to a sick man's only son they would be rather less than fair to him. If Charles Russell wrote to Sir Duncan Stoddart then Sir Duncan would telephone back again, and in any case the letter would be a difficult one to write.

Russell booked a call to Belfast, finishing dressing as he waited. When it came through he began to talk levelly. But not too levelly: if you sounded too casual people always assumed you had something to hide and mostly with good reason. Russell hid nothing but he didn't sound excited. At the end Stoddart said:

'Could it happen again?'

'It could happen in principle but I wouldn't see much point in it.'

'Is Neil being guarded?'

'Yes.'

'By corrupt local police? You're satisfied with that?' The voice was tired but it was a formidable voice still.

'By corrupt local police until today. I've a courier arriving later this morning and he's returning to London immediately. A man of my own will be leaving this evening.'

'Good.' Sir Duncan reflected for perhaps thirty shillings'-worth of a very expensive call. 'And why do you think they did it?'

'Pressure on you, your only son——'

There was a chuckle, amused but proud. 'That wasn't stupid in theory but in practice it was pointless. You know something?' Charles Russell denied he knew something. 'You'd got half-way through your story when I decided to recall Neil. So they'd worked it out right to that point; they've frightened me, *reached* me. But I've not recalled Neil and I'm not going to do so. You know why that is? He wouldn't come.'

'He's your son,' Russell said.

'Don't bank on blood where I'm concerned. I've not so long to live, I think, and there are things I value higher than a medium-haul aircraft. They got that bit quite right, you know. If they pushed me in a corner, the *Princess Rose* or Neil . . . Well, it hasn't come to that and you say it won't. I hope you're right. Meanwhile I can't thank you——'

'Don't try. I like Vittorio.'

Charles Russell hung up, finding that the courier was waiting for him. There was nothing of great importance. The Member for Boothetown East had been dining with the Military Attaché at an only nominally friendly embassy, but Russell wasn't worried by

114

the Member for Boothetown East. He was an earnest fellow-traveller but he was notoriously a wet one, and if Military Attachés wished to waste their *frais* on dining him Charles Russell had no objection. Now if it had been Tom Perivale . . .

Russell wrote brief instructions about the Member for Boothetown East and another and longer to his personal assistant. A top class guard was to be dispatched at once, one who could guarantee within reason that no mischief should befall his charge. He must speak adequate Italian, and recourse could be had to the outside list if there wasn't the right man available. He was to be sent immediately and was to report to Russell personally.

Russell dismissed the courier; he hadn't eaten breakfast and was hungry. He had no positive engagements, he was waiting the moves of other men, so he might as well break the day up. The Manin's resturant was excellent but one couldn't always eat there. He found a taxi and directed it to a *trattoria*. The driver had never heard of it and Russell explained its whereabouts. The driver suppressed a shrug. It was none of his business if well-to-do Englishmen chose to eat in a working quarter.

It was the café where Russell had spent an agreeable half-hour with a polite but talkative waiter. It was primarily a bar but at the back, behind bead curtains, Russell had noticed a handful of tables. Also that the tablecloths were spotless. It was the sort of *trattoria* where one either ate vilely or simply but very well.

He paid off the taxi and went in, humanly flattered that the waiter remembered him, not trying to hide his pleasure. There was lunch? But of course there was lunch—for a visitor the best. He was taken to a table and a plump little woman made first cousin to a curtsy. She followed it with a friendly smile—good teeth, Russell saw, and the southerner's splendid eyes. The signore desired? He desired to start with *pasta*. Russell didn't often eat it since he liked to keep his waistline, but today was an exception and he was courteous and considerate: if he ordered anything fancy they probably wouldn't have it, or they would think he was show-ing off, even trying to humiliate them. So *pasta* he said firmly to a face which beamed back instantly. But certainly—today was *cannelloni* day. Beautiful, made on the premises, not that rubbish from the grocer's. *Al dente*, superb. Very well, it was *cannelloni*. Then? Then there was veal. Charles Russell reflected that there was always veal. It wasn't his favourite meat, but handled properly it was edible. Could she get him a veal chop? Leave it on the bone of course, and do it fairly thoroughly. Peas and a green salad. If the signora would mix the dressing she'd do it very much better than he would. (This was untrue but also the lie permissible.) Another happy and flattered beam. To drink? A half-litre of red and a bottle of Recoardo. No Recoardo? Then San Pellegrino. *Subito, signore. Buon appetito.*

She bustled away.

Russell settled to eat with the appetite recommended, watching the bar through the looped bead curtains. Two other men had come into the dining-room, sitting behind him, taking their coats off to eat. They were talking in dialect and Russell caught little. He ate and watched the busy bar. Through the excellent *pasta* it had been no more than busy but with the chop it was suddenly crowded. Eight men had come in, one clearly the leader. He had taken off his overcoat and in the breast pocket of a sober suit there was a battery of fountain pens and pencils. Russell was sure he'd seen his face but he couldn't now place him. His manner too was interesting, something balanced between bonhomie and a half-concealed patronage. He was buying the drinks but he hadn't the air of celebrating. Unusual, worth watching . . .

Russell was suddenly conscious that the two men behind him had switched to bad German. He wasn't astonished that Italian work-men could speak German since thousands had had jobs in Germany and in Switzerland. What surprised him was that they wished to. He listened shamelessly.

'That's Pasquale Massaro.'

Pasquale Massaro—the man who'd brought that boy in up at SAGA! Angelo Franchin had called him Pasquale and he'd been wearing a row of fountain pens. Charles Russell had the face placed now, Charles Russell went on listening.

'Why isn't he working?'

'When you're high enough up in a union you can usually wangle off.'

'What's he doing in there?'

'Buying drinks for the faithful.'

'I don't like that, I don't at all. It's not our own union but one can't help hearing things. If that lot came out we should have to go along with them. Me, I've got kids and I like to see them eat.'

'Perhaps it won't happen.'

'Then why is he splashing the money round? I know two of the men with him and they're not just workmen.'

'Not to exaggerate. Pasquale's influential but he isn't a single boss. There's a committee and he's chairman——'

'Perhaps he's spending for himself.'

The other said unhappily: 'You may be right.'

They slipped back into dialect and Russell watched the bar again. So this was Pasquale Massaro, supervisor in SAGA, once candidate for an English job, reported by George Bailey to be ambitious in his union. It wasn't much to mark a man and nothing at all to hang on him. An ambitious committeeman buying drinks for his supporters. If this were England he'd be charging them.

Charles Russell settled his bill and rose. He was escorted to the door with protestations and some ceremony, leaving in a cosy cloud of mutual admiration. . . . He had eaten well? Of course he had. He'd come again? But certainly.

He took another bus which this time dropped him nearer to the Manin. As he went through the hall the porter handed him a letter. Renato Dagrappi would be grateful if Colonel Charles Russell could make a moment for a word with him. It was possible that Dagrappi had information which might be interesting. He could be found at via Vanda, Sixty-two, from half-past six and onwards. There was no need to reply if the suggestion was agreeable.

Charles Russell decided instantly. He'd been impressed by Dagrappi and the engagement would fill his evening. He looked up via Vanda on a street map the porter lent him. It seemed rather a prosperous area for an admitted working communist.

*

Dagrappi in turn had been impressed by Charles Russell. Renato wasn't a good golfer, but it hadn't been quite true when he'd insisted to Donnini that he played it only for the exercise. He knew no better test of men and Charles Russell had passed it. He had said he was Nine and perhaps he was, but at Rapallo he was unbeatable off that handicap. He wasn't long but nor was the course, and he had been hideously straight where length didn't matter; he'd pitched boldly past the hole and then attacked it; he hadn't left a putt short once. Neil Stoddart had offered him five shots in the eighteen holes but he hadn't come near conceding them. Russell had taken his pound with a happy smile, then spent it in the bar, and more, as happily. His pleasure had been infectious and they'd eaten with appetite. Charles Russell played to win and wasn't ashamed of it.

Dagrappi had liked him. He'd heard of Charles Russell and he knew what he did, so by definition he was an enemy to all communists. But it was a poor sort of communist who didn't recognize character when he saw it and a worse one indeed who'd disdain it for its difference. This man was an enemy, in the jargon a bourgeois jackal, but if jackals could be respectable Charles Russell demanded respect. This was a man whom a communist might do business with. Very limited business, naturally, but business nonetheless.

Renato had considered it carefully, for the situation in his absence had turned against him. He'd been afraid that it would, and his hour's steady telephoning had confirmed it. What he feared was a strike at SAGA. It was no part of his ethos that in a time of depression a strike would mean more unemployment. Nothing was born painlessly and the Italy he longed for would be certainly no exception. Personal suffering was irrelevant—you accepted that as a starting-point. But politics were immediate, and any strike would set him back a year.

And it would set him back much more if it were fought successfully. Dagrappi had all the communist's dislike of the orthodox unions, and for orthodox union leaders he had unlimited contempt. They were no better than tribal rainmakers, preposterous anachronisms making gestures as ineffective, acting out a ritual which preceded a natural event. They claimed cause and effect but had never established it. They never would since the connection was non-existent. They negotiated with the bosses and wages rose? Wages rose when employers must pay more to keep their labour. The well-fed faces round the table, the solemn platitudes of negotiation—absurd to suggest that these had influenced economics. It was worse than absurd, it was bad dialectic.

These men were Renato's enemies, enemies in principle and most of them in person, but he didn't yet want a clash with them. His party was infiltrating the unions but it didn't yet control the ones which mattered. Its power was outside—the cells, the network of information, the porters in the stark blocks of flats who could be father and mother to the families which lived in them. Most of these men were southerners and they'd imported their protest with them. They voted communist by instinct though few of them were Marxists. Most had never heard of him and even fewer wanted to. Renato's party too had power, a Tammany power to deliver a solid vote smoothly, but it hadn't yet mastered the major unions. Their leaders were self-seeking, many corrupt, and in any sort of pinch they had a horde of cassocked allies. Dagrappi had power, increasing power, but the time wasn't ripe for a head-on clash. When *he* called a strike it would be for something more than wages, the political action he'd been disciplined and trained for. In the meantime industrial action could only serve to weaken him and if it happened to be successful it could weaken him for some time.

So he didn't want a strike and nor did Russell. Renato had realized that at once. He was indifferent to the *Princess Rose*—the project was an international capitalist racket like another. But Russell would want her to fly on time and Russell now knew that there'd been several attempts to stop her. A strike might do that finally and there were rumours that one was brewing. It was true there was unemployment, but the cost of living was rising steadily and economic man was an abstraction of English economists. The workers were sheep, the shepherds ambitious and venal, men like Pasquale Massaro.

Renato Dagrappi loathed him.

Yes, a strike was a possibility and Charles Russell wouldn't want it. And nor would he stay in Vittorio if he felt himself quite power-less. The Executive was unique in its pragmatic English way. . . .

A bargain, Renato Dagrappi thought, the *combinazione* which both brain and his blood demanded. Charles Russell had passed the test of golf but Renato had another still. After all the man was English so one had to be quite certain that he wasn't a moralist too. Via Vanda would settle that neatly. If Russell were shocked, if he shook the dust off angrily, then he wasn't the man for Renato Dagrappi.

But if he didn't they'd do business.

Chapter Twelve

Russell took a taxi and arrived at via Vanda a little earlier than he'd intended to. It was a street of prosperous houses, of no merit architecturally but solid and comfortable. This was indeed a surprising area for an admitted working communist. Russell had expected to find that Number Sixty-two had been converted into flats but he saw there was only one bell. He rang it and waited.

The door was opened by a maid in cap and apron. . . . Signor Dagrappi had arrived yet? No, but he was expected. If the gentleman would come in. . . . The maid took Russell's hat and coat, leaving him in a well-proportioned room. It was soberly furnished in the taste of the turn of the century and had something of the air of a better club. Russell knew it was not. At a table in a corner four men had business papers out and a fifth was in a leather chair with a cigar which Russell envied. All were drinking champagne. From time to time a woman would walk in and out again, beautifully but severely dressed, her manner assured, a hostess waiting for a distinguished and expected guest, wishing to be sure he hadn't arrived without her knowledge. None of the men paid the least attention. Charles Russell shed twenty years in as many seconds. This was a champagne house and he ordered it.

The wine was better than he'd expected and he settled comfortably. He hadn't known they still existed. There'd been that stupid female Senator who'd destroyed the *maisons tolerées*, with the net result that honest prostitutes now lived at the end of a telephone. *Squilli*—the thought offended him. Protected and blackmailed—a shame. In any case this wasn't a *maison tolerée* but a house of the utmost distinction. Russell thought of his club without regret. It wasn't so dissimilar but the amenities were less catholic.

Presently an older woman came in, advancing at once on Russell. She tried him in German and, surprisingly, in French. Charles Russell could stumble along in both but said firmly that he was English. Then of course he'd be the gentleman whom her dear friend Dagrappi had asked her to look out for. Unfortunately she had no English. She was Greek herself.

Russell began to speak Greek to her. His Greek was most peculiar. To the classical tongue they'd beaten into him at school he had grafted in the war the demotic of the mountains where he'd fought. The hybrid was bizarre, even gently ridiculous, but Russell was Anglo-Irish and had none of the English inhibitions about languages. The average Englishman knew four times more French than he could contrive to get his tongue round: Charles Russell, on the contrary, spoke four times more Greek than he really knew.

Madam giggled but was enchanted. She led him to a sofa and the waiter changed the wine round; she accepted a glass gracefully. So he was the English Colonel whom Dagrappi had recommended to her. It was a pity about Renato's politics which were certainly not her own, nor, she imagined, an English Colonel's. No? That was good. But Dagrappi was a friend of hers and the Colonel was really welcome. She was delighted to see him since things weren't what once they had been. Not the same sort of client. . . . She flashed handsome dark eyes at the four men at the table. They were rich, she said sideways, but not, not——

She used a phrase which Russell knew. Its translation into English was a word which was unfashionable.

They chatted on in Charles Russell's astonishing Greek, sparring with mutual respect and sympathy. The Colonel would know the customs. A girl who wore a necklace had a previous engagement and had come into the room to announce she was at home. One had to do things decently and the old ways were the decent ones. But if she didn't have a necklace . . .

Charles Russell faced this splendid Greek. She might be forty-five but looked much less, still a warmly magnificent woman. He said softly that when one had reached a certain age one's tastes matured. They grew in fact discriminating, better.

Madam didn't answer but she poured more champagne; she raised her glass and smiled at him.

. . . Not immediately, alas. Pleasure was too important to mix with business.

Very prettily said, very handsome indeed. It was quieter after midnight too. What a pleasure to meet a *gentleman*. And now, if he'd forgive her, she must leave him for the moment. Madam rose with a girl's swift grace and smiled. Charles Russell bowed formally.

*

Renato Dagrappi arrived a minute later. Russell had always thought that Italian tailoring made a thickset race look even squatter than it was, good shoulders and heavy torso uneasily balanced on ugly legs, but Renato was taller than most and he carried his square-rigged suit with such elegance as it permitted. 'It was good of you to come,' he said.

'A pleasure.'

Dagrappi sat down, accepting the last of the bottle without exaggerated protest. He had made up his mind what to say to Russell, which was to tell him his own position and watch closely how Russell took it. He said simply that he was a communist of a certain influence in his party—Russell would know that already from Neil Stoddart—and that he was anxious that no strike should occur at SAGA. He was prepared to explain the reasons if Russell were interested but he believed that the fact would be sufficient, since Russell himself, though for different reasons, would have exactly the same anxiety. If that were correct they had much the same object, and a similar object was more important than differing ideologies.

Charles Russell had said that that was so, catching the waiter's eye, renewing the bottle. And what sort of strike did Dagrappi fear? For what reason, by whom organized?

'Have you heard of a man called Pasquale Massaro?'

'As it happens I have.'

Renato said respectfully: 'You're extremely well-informed.'

'Less well than you think. I know very little and quite by chance. My organization has to know a certain amount about what goes on in Vittorio, but it doesn't keep files on Vittorian personalities. All we know about Massaro is that he once tried to get work in England. We started the usual check on him but for some innocent reason the job didn't come off. Then when I came down here I mentioned his name to a contact of mine. He told me that Massaro was a supervisor at SAGA and that he was influential in his union and moreover ambitious. That's all I know of him.'

'I could tell you much more.' Renato Dagrappi did so. It wasn't the picture of an attractive or upright man. Russell listened, impressed; at the end he said quietly:

'I should tell you I've met him.'

'Met him?' Dagrappi was surprised and didn't hide it.

'Seen him would be more accurate. Today as it happens. I was eating in a part of the town I like and Pasquale Massaro came into the bar of the *trattoria*. I knew it was him because two men behind me said it was. They also said what you are—that a strike was a

124

possibility. Massaro was buying drinks all round. They didn't like that either.'

'You get around,' Dagrappi said.

'You mustn't think I'm the great detective. What I really do here is wait. I wait for the moves of other men and sometimes when I'm lucky I save a little from the wreck. But I'm strictly on the defensive—that's implicit since I'm a foreigner.'

'If I may ask it—the local police co-operate?'

Russell said blandly: 'The local police have local difficulties.'

'That I can understand; I'm not a foreigner.' Dagrappi considered. 'You wait for the moves of other men——'

'Let me save you the question.' Russell had made his mind up; he'd string along with Dagrappi since he hadn't another ally. After all, he thought ironically, it wouldn't be the first time. Communism frightened him but not a good communist. One needed a long spoon no doubt, but Russell wasn't without experience. He returned to Renato. 'You'll know about the *Princess Rose* and you'll know that there's been trouble up at SAGA. The papers haven't carried all of it but enough to draw the outline, and if you're what I think you are you'll have the sources to fill it in. So there've been delays to the *Rose*'s schedule and then two attempts at sabotage. We don't think the motive comes from Vittorio or even Italy, but the operator is in this town, I'm sure.' Charles Russell turned directly to Dagrappi. 'Have you heard of a man called Luthman?'

'I've heard of Carl Luthman and of plenty of others like him. He's a rich business man who's made a fortune out of Vittorians.' Dagrappi smiled. 'Anathema, of course.'

Russell said dryly: 'I note the gesture.'

'But it was more than a reflex.' Dagrappi drank some wine, considering. 'With respect,' he said finally, 'it doesn't make sense.'

'You're the professional dialectician—shoot it down.'

'Then somebody, not Italian, wants to sabotage your *Rose*. I accept that without question and I can make my own guess who's behind it. What I accept less easily is that they'd hire a rich Swede as saboteur.'

Russell looked at Dagrappi with increasing respect. 'But I'd thought of that myself.'

'Then how do you fit it in, please?'

'I don't think Carl Luthman is merely a hired agent. I think he started as a fixer—the delays to the *Rose*'s schedule and perhaps the first sabotage—but I believe he raised the fire himself. That only makes sense if he were more than a straight agent. But if he had a direct and personal interest——'

'Such as shares or a percentage?'

Russell said coolly: 'You'd have made a good capitalist.'

'Of course I should. I could have made a fortune if I'd wanted to. Any educated communist could do that.'

Charles Russell didn't comment. The statement was preposterous but had a simplicity which appealed to him. Besides, it might be true. But Dagrappi was apeaking again: 'So accepting that Luthman's behind all this, what are you going to do?'

'I told you—I have to wait for his moves.'

'That isn't satisfactory.'

'If you've any suggestions——'

'Only the obvious. Remove this Luthman.'

'I'm a foreign official on another man's patch. I'm quite without standing. I admit I have certain resources but I don't think they'd cover the removal of a Vittorian.'

'You misunderstand me.' Dagrappi stared at his pointed shoes. 'I was thinking of ourselves,' he said.

Charles Russell was silent but quite unastonished. Communism was a state within a state. There was also another and its officials wore black. That made three in one country. Italian life must be uncomfortably complicated but then it always had been. Russell hated complication and he began to speak deprecatingly: 'I doubt if the moment's quite ripe for removals. There'd be time to arrange another agent and we'd be fumbling in the dark again.' If Renato noticed the plural he didn't show it. Charles Russell went on. 'It's very unsatisfactory to be defending, but at least we know our enemy. Remove him and we lose even that.'

'I take the point.' Dagrappi thought again. 'What I'm fearing is a strike,' he said, 'and if it came it would be Massaro's strike. There are plenty of rumours, plenty of unrest, and if Luthman latches on to them——'

'You mean contact Massaro? You mean offer him money? From what you tell me I gather he'd do most things for money.'

Renato Dagrappi nodded.

'Do you know if they're connected or even if they've met?'

'I mean to find that out at once.'

'I don't doubt you can.' Charles Russell reflected. 'So there's the climate for a strike and you know of a man who might call one. That would be for reasons unconnected with the *Rose*—ambition first and then money if it's offered. And I know of a man who would also like a strike because, at this moment, it would just about finish her. Let's suppose the position hardens, that there's a positive threat of this strike we don't want——'

He left it unfinished because Renato had interrupted him. Russell wasn't offended since he knew the Italian habit. Once a meaning was clear the main clause was irrelevant. Renato was saying: 'You're asking me what I could do? I'll show you.'

Russell let it pass again for this was another habit. When words would be difficult, apt to be embarrassing or simply misinterpreted, one showed. Donnini had shown him, he'd shown Donnini. Now Dagrappi wished to show him too and it was unlikely to be un-interesting. Charles Russell rose and the waiter brought a bill to him. Russell pulled out his pocketbook but the waiter shook his head. He had very firm instructions about the bill. The signore could sign it but no money would be accepted. Charles Russell signed and Renato smiled. He had already been happy that he could do business with this Englishman, but he hadn't expected to find him signing the bill in via Vanda quite so quickly.

They took a taxi to the quarter which Russell was beginning to regard as his own discovery, stopping outside a block of flats, dismissing the taxi; they went to the porter's flat and Renato began to talk to him. He was a small dark man, but thick-set and powerful, evidently a southerner. He answered Renato in dialect, but Renato explained that his friend was English—the porter must speak Italian if he could. The porter tried. It wasn't good but Russell could follow some of it. The woman in Forty-seven was shortly due to pup again and last time she'd nearly died of it. She couldn't get into hospital, her man wasn't working. . . . Renato made a note of it. And talking of not working there were frightening rumours about a strike. Dagrappi said simply that the party deplored a strike.

That was all right, then.

Not to be too sure of it. The enemy was powerful.

They went on to another block, the same southern porter, the cups of strong coffee. Here it was number Twenty-two. The police were after him on some trumped-up charge. . . .

Really trumped-up? One had to know to be useful.

'Well' . . .

Renato made another note, he'd see about a lawyer.

They moved on to two cafés, a shop and a sort of club. The same welcome at all, the same matter-of-fact disposal of petty business. Petty but to these people vital. Peasants two years or less ago, many semi-illiterate, where could they turn in the jungle that was Vittorio if not to friends? Renato was their friend, Renato's party. It didn't harangue them, it greased the wheels. In this alien scaring city they needed greasing for the simple.

When they left the club Renato hesitated. It was his intention to ask Charles Russell to dinner, but he was carrying little money since like all utterly dedicated men, priest or committed communist, he was content to live on what kept him alive to serve. The five thousand lire which was all he had would hardly dine Russell in the manner he was accustomed to. Or so Renato feared. He approached the matter crabwise.

'I think you said you'd seen Pasquale Massaro in the bar of a *trattoria*?'

'Not a stone's throw from here. It's called Da Nico.'

Renato's fears were at once removed. 'You can certainly pick them. It's the best of its kind for miles. I'd be honoured if you'd have supper there. I know Nico too—he's another of my friends.'

'I've taken the point that you've plenty of friends.'

They began to walk briskly, silent with their respective thoughts. Russell's were simple: he'd been shown once again and had drawn his own conclusions. He was confident they were the right ones. Renato couldn't stop a strike, or not in the sense that he could prevent a trade union calling one, but he clearly controlled the grassroots—people. They might not actually scab in a formal strike but they wouldn't fight with gusto if Renato advised them not to. He could do things if he decided to, and would.

They went into Da Nico, received with something like astonishment. The *padrone*'s wife was flattered but kept staring at Dagrappi. He wasn't the kind of company she'd expected of an Englishman. Her husband came out from behind the bar and Renato introduced him. He offered no explanation and none was asked, but Russell caught an undertone exchange.

'Massaro's here. He's eating inside with three or four others.'

'That won't disturb my appetite.'

'You might disturb Massaro's.'

'Good.'

'But he's my customer, you know, besides our enemy.'

'Are you suggesting we eat elsewhere?' Dagrappi was smiling but his voice had an edge.

'You know I'm not. I'm saying I have a living to earn.'

Renato didn't answer. They went into the dining-room through the looped bead curtains. Two tables had been put together and Pasquale's party was sitting at them. There were three two-litre bottles of wine, two of them empty, and a meal not quite finished. Russell and Dagrappi sat down at another table. For a moment nothing happened, then Massaro put money down. He rose without a word and the others rose with him. They filed out in silence, Massaro leading. None of them looked at Renato Dagrappi.

He said to Charles Russell: 'You see?'

'I see.'

*

They finished their dinner and this time telephoned for a taxi. Russell looked at his watch; he was free until midnight and suggested a nightcap at the Manin. Renato accepted, and they were in the comfortable bar when the porter came up with a letter for Russell. It had been left with instructions that it be delivered to him personally.

'You'll excuse me?'

'Of course.'

Russell opened the sealed envelope. There was a brief note from Mario Donnini on headed paper and signed, and a single sheet of foolscap, typed and without letterhead or signature. Russell read it carefully, for it was a complete report on Carl Luthman's movements since his return to Vittorio. He had been going to his office as usual but he hadn't been using his car, nor had he sent it for repairs. That was only to be expected and no positive conclusions could be drawn from what was negative. His movements had been normal except for one. He'd called at a foreign consulate and it hadn't been his own.

Charles Russell concealed a smile. Correctitude paid, a proper consideration for the feelings of fellow officials. He'd sent Neil Stoddart straight to Donnini with that incendiary and now Mario was reciprocating. Later they'd reached an understanding about Carl Luthman and the Commissario was demonstrating that he intended to keep it strictly. Charles Russell considered, said finally to Dagrappi: 'You asked me whether the local police co-operated about Carl Luthman. I ducked the question and I'm still obliged to duck it. In terms, that is. But I've something here which I'd like to show you. No questions, though.' He folded the sheet of foolscap to show only the last paragraph, handing it to Renato. It wasn't a gesture he would have risked with every Italian.

He hadn't expected it would produce the effect it did. Dagrappi began to laugh, its note less amusement than a solid satisfaction. He'd been back in Vittorio for a night and a day and he hadn't been interfered with by the police. Now he knew he wouldn't be —his assessment of the situation had been correct. It had been an inference that Donnini was in a difficulty but it had been a gamble that it would be the sort of difficulty which would inhibit action against himself. And now it was clear it was. Mario and this cool Englishman were in this SAGA affair together, they were in fact co-operating actively. And he was a friend of Charles Russell's, or at least it would be known they'd been in contact. Mario was a competent policeman and he'd know by now that Renato had returned. He was probably being shadowed so they'd know he'd met Charles Russell. That man at the bar had all the smell of a plain clothes copper. He was comfortably out of earshot but he'd have plenty to report: Dagrappi and Colonel Russell had spent an evening together—excellent.

Next move to Donnini and he wouldn't risk a wrong one.

Dagrappi said in apology: 'I'm afraid it's very rude to have private jokes.'

'It's also understandable.'

'May I ask what you deduce from this?'

'Personally I was making the assumption that Carl Luthman is behind our troubles—first as a fixer, then later, I think, as an active operator. That is still an assumption and you don't have to make the same one.'

'But I will.'

'Thank you . . . So Luthman has gone to a consulate—not his own consulate but that of the country which has an established commercial interest in destroying the *Princess Rose*. I mean destroying her commercially which covers physical destruction too. But I think they'd have risked the latter only if they'd been desperate. They *have* risked it—they're in a hurry.'

Renato said thoughtfully: 'You think a consulate would help him in actual crime?'

'Yes and no. They wouldn't assist him actively, or not in anything which could be traced to them, but they'd provide, well, facilities.'

'You're serious?'

'Perfectly. We're dealing with one of the most powerful industries in the world, and it wouldn't at all surprise me if somebody in this consulate had personal motive to oblige it. Why not? These men aren't Englishmen—they're a vigorous, young and competitive people. I emphasize competitive.' Charles Russell paused. 'You mustn't think,' he added smoothly, 'that I'm presuming to judge them. I simply state the facts which I've observed. Judgements, in my profession, are mostly fatal.'

'You don't surprise me.' Dagrappi's voice was dry but his face approving.

'Then how do you see this new development yourself?'

'In much the same way but from my own point of view. What I fear is a strike at SAGA, and the man I'm afraid might call one is Pasquale Massaro. Now evidently your Luthman is being watched by the police, and on the story you've told me so far I'd say he probably suspects he is. It's possible he *knows* it. One does, you'll agree, there's a certain sixth sense . . .' Renato dropped his voice a tone. 'That man at the bar is a plain clothes nark.'

Charles Russell flicked a glance at him. 'You're right,' he said. 'Watching you, I suppose.'

'Hardly Colonel Charles Russell.'

'It would be possible but for reasons I mustn't tell you most improbable. Where were we in your argument?'

'At the point where Carl Luthman suspects he's being watched. Suspects is good enough as a hypothesis because if he even suspects the fact he wouldn't dare contact Massaro. Not directly, that is. But if he has a contact in a consulate they could talk through it, pass money. Pasquale may be hesitating, waiting the perfect moment to call a strike which is certainly on. But offer Pasquale money to force it *now*. . . . You think I'm talking rubbish about the consulate?'

'Very far from it. It's just the sort of contact I had in mind in the word facilities.' Charles Russell raised his glass. 'I said earlier this evening you were a professional logician. I was joking, I apologize. I repeat the statement now and I do not joke.'

Dagrappi bowed and Charles Russell again reflected; he said finally, choosing his words, risking a hint of weightiness which he wouldn't ordinarily have accepted: 'I've certain facilities of my own in this city but they don't extend to putting a shadow on a trade union leader whom we both have different reasons to be afraid of.'

'That is my side, my Colonel.'

'Right.'

Dagrappi rose, writing on an envelope. 'That's my number at my flat.'

'And I'm usually here.'

'Then may I make a suggestion? Stay in central Vittorio. Keep out of the working quarters. Don't eat again where we ate tonight.'

'Why ever not?' Charles Russell was at last astonished.

'May I answer with another question? Carl Luthman will know you're here?'

133

'Of course.'

'Does Pasquale Massaro?'

'I can't possibly say he doesn't.'

'He's seen you, you know—today and perhaps before. You're rather a famous person, not the sort a man would want walking around if he were planning trouble against your interest. And a strike is against your interest.'

'I can see what you're hinting but I'm sure you exaggerate.'

Dagrappi looked at Russell and checked a shrug; he smiled and held his hand out. 'To our next pleasant meeting.'

'To our next fruitful meeting.'

Renato took a bus and went back to Da Nico. It was shut but he was admitted. He went with the *padrone* into the empty dining-room; he talked for some time and the *padrone* nodded. Pasquale Massaro was to be tailed and his movements reported. It was possible but unlikely that he would visit a certain consulate, but it was probable that he had a contact there. This contact would be a go-between between Massaro and a most dangerous man called Luthman. The real contact at the consulate wouldn't show himself —he'd use somebody at two or three removes, almost certainly an Italian. So if Pasquale was seen talking to anybody unusual it would be interesting. If money was seen to pass it would be final. That was properly understood? Passing money to Pasquale would be conclusive.

And there was something else. Renato Dagrappi took a sip of the inevitable coffee. It would keep him awake but it couldn't be refused without offence. Renato was uneasy. This distinguished English administrator of what was perhaps the most famous counter-espionage organization in the world. . . . He was astonishingly young in mind but he was middle-aged in person. Luthman's going to that consulate could mean more than contacting Pasquale or even passing money to him. It was that almost certainly but on Russell's own assessment of the commercial powers and interests involved. . . . He mightn't quite realize that in a city like Vittorio . . .

Renato gave instructions again, and again Nico nodded.

*

When Dagrappi had left him Charles Russell looked at the time. It was a quarter to twelve and madam had impressed on him that it was quieter after midnight. He had an appointment which he meant to keep. He telephoned for a taxi and directed it back to via Vanda.

He left next morning at half-past nine after an English breakfast which madam herself had cooked for him. He had eaten it ravenously in a dressing-gown she had found for him, then shaved and bathed in elegance, even luxury. The maid had conducted him out, then shut the door. He stood in the crisp morning air, relaxed, feeling forty. He decided to walk and had taken two steps when he stopped. It couldn't be true but he didn't doubt his senses. Somebody was tailing him.

Charles Russell chuckled. This hadn't happened to him for longer than he cared to think about, but the sensation wasn't displeasing. And it was somehow appropriate, another and a master's touch to this shiningly youthful morning. He was genuinely unfrightened, though he wasn't a man who was stranger to normal fear. None of the orthodox things was happening: his spine wasn't crawling, the hair on his nape lay flat. Nevertheless he knew.

He sniffed the air like an animal and, equally unthinkingly, looked around the solid street. There were one or two pedestrians, respectable business men walking to their offices for the exercise. None of them gave him a glance, no sinister figures lurked in doorways. But the curtains of these prosperous houses were still mostly drawn, and behind any of them. . . .

Charles Russell began to laugh aloud. Dagrappi had been babbling about his staying in central Vittorio, about not going up to Da Nico again. The man had been exaggerating and Russell had asked him not to, but there was a sort of contagious fever which the underworld passed unconsciously—suspicion, the over-insurance of risks which were seldom worth the premium. So Dagrappi was keeping an eye on him. He might honestly fear for Russell's safety at other hands, but it was equally likely that he was covering himself against the chance of an English treachery. That he was entitled to—Russell wasn't offended. His opinion of Dagrappi rose higher than ever.

He lit a cigar, reflecting that the only failing in an otherwise admirable woman was that madam couldn't stand cigar smoke. He'd had to make do with cigarettes—he could smoke them but not too many. He looked round the solid street again, half-imagining that a curtain had twitched. He knew that it hadn't but he waved at it blithely. Then he walked away briskly, smoking.

. . . They were serious men these communists, good men to work with.

Chapter Thirteen

Russell returned to the Manin still hungry. He seriously considered a second breakfast but decided against it since he was lunching with Neil Stoddart and it was a meal he was looking forward to. He wasn't disposed to spoil an appetite.

They sat down together quietly and Russell listened. Six sentences told him what he'd more than half hoped to find: Neil Stoddart had matured. He had always been tough-minded but in a sense a little simple. To Charles Russell the word was by no means pejorative. It was good to be simple when the character lay behind it, but it was better to be experienced. A single incident could do it. It needn't be a traumatic one but its impact could be decisive. Neil Stoddart had been an efficient young executive. Now he was a man.

And he'd been talking to his father on equal terms. He hadn't put it like that to Russell but Russell had sensed it at once. They'd decided together and he thought they'd decided well. The programme for the *Rose* had been put forward not put back; she was to show her paces in forty-eight hours and they'd asked the world to watch her. There was nothing against it mechanically, the engines were in and she'd broken the back of her trials in semi-secrecy, but of course there were disadvantages. She wasn't fitted yet for passengers or for any of the lay-outs which were standard, nor was there much behind her in production. That was more serious, since possible buyers would ask firm dates. The original plan had been to hold back the formal launching till the prototype was backed by the certainty of delivery—six finished within a month at most, then a calculated flow as the production line spawned *Roses*. That was the normal way to time it but the situation wasn't normal. The new programme was a risk which they'd been forced to accept, and what had been decisive had been the redoubling of the smear campaign. They had to give the lie to that: the *Rose* could fly, the *Rose* flew well. So they'd sent out the invitations and, since Stoddart's weren't quite children in what was tiresomely called public relations, they were also busily hinting at the reason why they'd advanced the date. That hint was the truth, and on the whole it had been well received. There were plenty of buyers of aircraft more than a little angry at the methods of those who sold them.

Neil Stoddart accepted a glass of wine but left it. . . . So it was very short notice but they'd had no important refusals yet. They were playing the thing for sympathy and from many they were getting it. That hadn't been quite surprising but it was gratifying too. It was Tuesday today and on Thursday at half eleven they'd take the covers off. Sir Duncan himself was coming down, alas by train but the doctors had insisted. The rest of the board would fly, as would all the prospective buyers. SAGA would lunch the big boys afterwards. The offices of the aircraft division had been burnt down, so they'd use the main building in Vittorio itself. Lunch for the heavyweights in the boardroom and in hotels for the rest. Most of the local brass, cars for two hundred people. An occasion—they'd splash it. Colonel Russell would come to the boardroom, of course. If he hadn't come down here there probably wouldn't be a *Rose* to show. And she could do it, the *Rose*, that *Rose* could *fly*. The *Princess Rose* . . .

Russell let him talk on, listening at two levels. At one this was the talk of a matured and confident man, but Russell was experienced and he wasn't quite satisfied. He began to probe delicately: 'This is very good news.'

'It means we've a chance still.'

It was a very long way from the affirmative expected. The probe had been justified and Russell pushed at it again. 'If you've only a chance then there's also a chance against you.'

'Yes.'

There was a silence and Russell waited; finally he had to break it himself. 'If there's anything I can do . . .'

'God knows you've done enough for us, but I'd ask for more if I thought you could help. But this is domestic—inside SAGA.'

Russell said softly: 'A strike?'

'How on earth did you know?'

'There've been rumours of a strike for weeks.'

'I see.' Neil Stoddart sounded doubtful but didn't press it. 'A strike would finish the *Rose*,' he said, 'before Thursday or even afterwards. Before would be worse but after would kill her too. We've got to deliver or at least to be seen to be able to.'

Charles Russell considered, at last took a chance on it. 'I've been here a week and I'm not without connections now.'

'I'm sure you're not. *I* am.'

'I don't think I follow.'

For the first time Neil Stoddart drank a mouthful of wine. 'There's a *case* for a strike. These men work well, the cost of living has been rising, and if we get only half the orders for the *Princess Rose* we hope to we could stand a modest increase. You know what would happen in England. They'd ask for two bob and we'd offer a tanner. Somewhere about a shilling we'd reach terms.'

'Then why not do just that?'

'Because of the man who's succeeded Franchin. His name doesn't matter since he's married to a Monti, and he's absolutely adamant —no rise.'

'That's odd,' Russell said, 'in the circumstances you tell me.'

'Odd? I wish I thought so.' Neil Stoddart leant forward. 'The aircraft company at SAGA is only part of the Monti empire. It's what we've put Stoddart money in but it's butter to the Montis, not their bread. This man's married to a Monti, close to the old man himself. If he's sticking on a rise then you can take it the Montis are sticking.'

'But why? With the *Princess Rose* at the crossroads——'

'They may not care for the *Princess Rose*, they may have decided that she's expendable. She's one interest in many others and if they're looking at all the others they could very well expend her.' Neil Stoddart drew a deliberate breath. 'I'm afraid they may really, *want* a strike.'

'I'm repeating myself. . . . But why again?'

'You've been here a week and you've been here before; you have marvellous information on almost everything. So you'll know this isn't England, nor is the northern Italian industrialist like an English tycoon. He doesn't treat men too badly, he's much less of an exploiter than the communists make out, but he's essentially paternal. He resents the trade unions because he's never learnt to live with them. He's an old-fashioned father, not unfair and some-times generous, but he'll fight like a devil if he feels his position's threatened. There's a good deal of unemployment, the moment may look a good one for a showdown . . .'

They had been interrupted by a waiter with an envelope. Neil Stoddart apologized and opened it; he passed the contents to Russell.

'A meeting at three with the representatives of the metal-workers?'

Neil Stoddart nodded.

'Expected?'

'No.'

Russell asked quietly: 'Is Pasquale Massaro a metalworker?'

'You know him?'

'I've heard the name.'

'You hear a lot, you really do.'

'You said I had good sources . . . So is Massaro a metalworker?'

'Yes, and an influential one. On the whole he holds the yea or nay.'

'He'll be at this meeting?'

'Yes.' Neil Stoddart rose. 'And now if you'll excuse me, sir.'

'Of course. And I'm always here.'

Russell went back to his room and undressed. He had earned his afternoon nap, and twice. He considered Pasquale Massaro in the minute before sleep came to him. If what Neil believed about the Montis' plans was true then Pasquale Massaro was a man with his head in a considered and well-baited trap. Such men were seldom dangerous, certainly not dangerous enough to deprive a middle-aged but still vigorous security officer of his siesta. Charles Russell, half asleep by now, was inclined to write Pasquale off.

*

Carl Luthman was not since he hadn't another weapon now. He'd been in contact with Pasquale since the original plan to delay the *Rose*. A strike would have delayed her if Dr Franchin had failed to, and he'd chosen to work through the Doctor first because his contact was more direct with him. Then they'd pushed him brutally into sabotage and sabotage had failed in turn. Moreover and worse it had frightened Pasquale. Carl Luthman had telephoned when he'd returned from the motorway and Pasquale had cold-shouldered him. Some ridiculous condition about eliminating an English Colonel . . .

It had shaken Carl Luthman but he'd thought it over coolly. It was bluff, he'd decided, an outsize bluff. Pasquale liked power but Pasquale loved money—they wouldn't have been in contact if his reputation had been otherwise—and now he was stepping his price up. He could do it at that, he held Luthman helpless. This might be a bluff but Carl Luthman couldn't call it; he couldn't because he had nothing else left. So he'd have to pay more and he hated all paying.

He took a taxi to a consulate, finding what he'd expected there, a man who would listen. It had been quite a junior officer but connected with trade promotion. He'd had an acquisitive nose and sharp dark eyes and he heard out Carl Luthman with mounting interest. . . . So Luthman knew Garnett Anderson?

Yes.

And he wished to convey a message on Garnett Anderson's behalf?

He did.

To a man called Pasquale Massaro who might not wish to be seen with Luthman?

That was so.

It could also be understandable. And there had been mention of money.

Ten million lire for a service already discussed.

The sharp-eyed man had worked it out. Even in dollars that was still sixteen big ones. That was Garnett Anderson money, and Anderson was a man he'd very willingly oblige. When he went back to the States again. . . .

'You want this money conveyed?' he asked.

'No, only that it's available. One half on acceptance, the other on completion.'

'Right. I can fix it to give that message and I will. Leave your address and number, please.'

And now the answer had come back to him from the consulate. Massaro wouldn't budge an inch; he'd mentioned a certain

Englishman for he'd known of his arrival. But now he'd actually seen him and in company which scared him stiff. There was a meeting at SAGA this afternoon but it wouldn't be the final one. The proposal was on but the terms were unchanged. No strike till this Englishman had been eliminated.

. . . So it hadn't been bluff, the damned man had meant it.

Luthman had writhed again but he'd returned to the consulate. This time sharp-eyes interrupted him. 'You're asking a wicked lot,' he said. 'This is crime and I'm not a criminal.'

'I'm asking for Garnett Anderson.'

'I know you are—I believe you too. I might very well not have but we've certain information about an aircraft.' Sharp-eyes tapped massive dentures with a pencil. 'I can't possibly help you directly but I'll give you a name. He'll give you another, and maybe there'll be a third behind. And if the job comes unstuck and you mention me. . . .' The dark eyes went suddenly black as night. 'You'll remember that this is Vittorio.'

'I quite understand. I'm grateful.'

'Good.' Sharp-eyes wrote a name and number in block capitals in Luthman's notebook. 'He's sometimes arranged odd jobs for us. In no circumstances go to see him—that's for your sake, not mine. And use a public telephone.'

Half an hour later Russell was reading another report from the Commissario. He had been woken for its delivery. Carl Luthman had called a second time at the consulate previously mentioned.

That was interesting, Charles Russell thought, but it didn't advance the story. Something was cooking between Carl Luthman and Massaro, and the consulate was the go-between. Almost certainly it was about this strike, but one visit or six they wouldn't know till it broke.

He yawned and went back to sleep again. He felt he was entitled to.

★

Renato Dagrappi had been meticulously trained, and behind the careful training lay the instincts of a commander. He liked to check and was doing so now, ringing to Da Nico from his flat.

Had anything come in yet about Pasquale?

No, not yet.

No unusual contacts?

Nothing seen. His telephone had been ringing more than usual and there was a meeting up at SAGA at three o'clock.

No money seen to pass to him?

Almost certainly not by hand.

Renato said slowly: 'Then we've a little more time—not much.'

'For what?'

'To prevent him acting foolishly. To stop a disaster we none of us want. And talking of disaster there's that Englishman Colonel Russell——'

'Your instructions are being carried out.'

'Day and night?'

'Night and day.'

*

Russell woke refreshed at five o'clock. His rest had been longer than what he normally regarded as a siesta, but he had none of the English instinct that to sleep in the day was wicked. He took a bath and changed his shirt for he was going to via Vanda again. He was a man of middle age but without delusions that he was young still; he was going to via Vanda because he hadn't another engagement, nor a club in Vittorio to pass an idle evening in. Via Vanda was his surrogate club and Charles Russell thought it a good one. So he'd use its facilities though not, tonight, all of them.

He paid off his taxi and climbed the steps. Another car had slowed behind him, then driven on a yard or two and stopped. Two men were getting out of it. Charles Russell rang the bell and turned. The men had left the empty car, mounting the steps behind him, moving with a deliberate menace. Russell blinked incredulously. The men were masked and their right hands were in the pockets of black overcoats.

Colonel Charles Russell was too astonished to feel much fear. Later he realized that he'd been humanly frightened, but for the moment he felt disbelief. Men with masks and presumably weapons! This was Saturday evening on I.T.A., not life. Deplorably it was, though—the men were moving in on him. He still stood above them but the advantage wasn't a useful one. He supposed he could kick, even that queer two-footed kick he'd watched on the goggle-box, but they were two to one and if he missed the steps would break his back. These men could do that in any case. Charles Russell stood still and waited. The first man had a cosh out now and Russell rolled with the blow. He rolled a little too far and fell. The first man stumbled over him and the second across the first.

. . . Disgracefully unprofessional.

There was a flurry of ill-directed blows as the men reached their feet again. Russell stayed crouched. Only one blow had counted and his hat had taken some of it. The street door opened on a gaping maid and Russell rolled backwards through it. The maid was in hysteria now but Charles Russell kicked the door shut.

He pulled himself upright shakily, shooting the bolt. There was a judas, he saw, and he opened it cautiously. A second car had drawn up and four men had emerged from it. They ran up the steps and these four were professionals. It was over in seconds, hardly a fight at all. Four men were carrying two to a big saloon. They threw them inside and jumped in themselves. The saloon roared away.

Charles Russell walked unsteadily to the room he'd been shown to earlier. There were curious glances but no comment at all. This was a club whose members minded their own business. Just like his own in London. He found an armchair and gave the waiter instructions. His arrival was to be announced to madam, please. Yes, that was all.

When she found him he was unconscious.

Chapter Fourteen

He woke next morning in a room which he saw at once was not a hospital's. He was in a comfortable double bed but it wasn't the one he'd used before. There were elaborate curtains and a woman's dressing-table cleared of impedimenta, and he was wearing pyjamas which weren't his own. He had a confused recollection of having vomited disgracefully, of madam, experienced and composed in crisis, and of a doctor who had given him an injection. Italian doctors, he remembered, were slightly dotty about injections. There was a lump on his head and he supposed he'd been concussed, but he hadn't a headache; he felt tired but his mind was clear.

Russell began to cast the balance of the previous evening's events. He hadn't been seriously damaged but inescapably he'd been wounded, and the wound was to his *amour propre* since he'd been guilty of grave misjudgement. It had stemmed from modesty rather than arrogance but it had still been misjudgement. He simply hadn't credited that Charles Russell, a foreigner, a man without powers either legal or local, could be a worthwhile target in Vittorio. Dagrappi had thought otherwise, and if he'd known him a little better Russell would have laughed at him. And Dagrappi had been right and Russell wrong.

Charles Russell sighed. He knew very well that he was sometimes guarded. He had never suggested it but had been conscious of the occasions. In London, for instance, and always in Washington. In the latter it had been obvious but in London unobtrusive. His personal assistant had put a well-trained man on him, and there had certainly been circumstances when the action had been reasonable. Twice it had been justified. But here in a foreign country the head of the Executive wasn't a target. Or so he had thought and wrongly. It was the mistake which flicked his self-esteem—on other counts he was innocent. This wasn't a case of a middle-aged administrator stupidly deciding that he was young enough for an active role, but he was supposed to be experienced, he was paid to use his judgement, and his judgement had failed him badly. He'd put a guard on Neil Stoddart even though Donnini had put on one of his own already, but himself he hadn't thought for. Wrong. Modest perhaps, but indubitably wrong. What was more, Renato had warned him.

For the first time he smiled. At least he hadn't sought the thing, he hadn't stuck his neck out. Not like old Withers. George Withers was a General, a member of Russell's club, and one night he'd woken with a burglar standing over him. George Withers was seventy but he'd promptly attacked the burglar, and they'd found him next morning rather badly beaten up. He'd been two months in hospital and had been dining on the story for two years. Plenty of people thought the General a hero: Charles Russell considered him a foolish old man.

He turned his head to the night table. There was a postcard propped against the telephone, words printed on it in capitals. They said RING WHEN WOKEN and Russell did so.

Madam herself came in, smiling and calm, underplaying the moment with native tact. This admirable establishment for which

148

there wasn't a word in England because it didn't exist there might have been organized expressly as a refuge for middle-aged security officers who, by their own misjudgement, had been attacked on its doorstep. She didn't ask questions, she didn't fuss. Instead she said pleasantly: 'The doctor's calling again later but he says you'll be quite all right. By tomorrow at worst. You've had mild concussion—you're not to drink. But you can eat what you like and I dare say you're hungry.'

'I don't know how to apologize, I——'

She waved it aside magnificently. 'You're my guest.'

'I'm a tiresome old nuisance.'

'Not old—experienced.'

'I haven't been displaying it.'

For an instant she hesitated. 'Renato's told me who you are.'

'That makes you the kinder.'

'You fought in my country, we pay our debts. Are you ready for breakfast?'

'Really, I——'

She didn't answer but left him, returning with a tray. There were coffee and rolls, eggs and bacon and marmalade. 'You liked it before.' She sat down on the bed. 'And by the way, you've a visitor when you've finished your breakfast. The doctor says you're not to move till he's checked you, but you can see a visitor if you want to.'

'Who's the visitor?'

'Dagrappi.'

'Yes, I want to see Renato.'

'I guessed you might.' She fished in a pocket, producing a carton of Italian cigars. 'We had to look in your coat and your money's in the safe. I dare say these aren't your mark at all but your cigar case was empty.'

'You're going to let me smoke cigars?' Charles Russell was surprised but touched.

'You're our most distinguished invalid. We've had others for other reasons—' her grimace defined the reasons—'but I didn't regard them as friends.'

She smiled and went away again, and ten minutes later Renato Dagrappi came in. He took a chair by the bed and began almost casually.

'I thought you might want to talk to me.'

Russell didn't immediately answer. He was thinking that Englishmen had a fairly general impression about Italians: they were wildly unreliable, you could never finish a sentence, they were tricky about money, calculating. . . . All this was true but they were other things too. They had, for instance, delicacy, the natural aplomb of an ancient and invariably surviving race. Renato hadn't come to reprove him—what had happened had happened. So had invasions, the Papal States, Napoleon, Normans, Austrians and Spaniards—the people had survived the lot. Renato sat by his bed and waited; Renato Dagrappi smiled.

Russell said softly: 'I've made a foolish mistake, I've caused unnecessary trouble. You warned me, too. I'm sorry.'

'*Uffa.*' The smile was a tolerant grin. 'And now?'

'I'm English with English weaknesses. Let's start at the beginning.'

'I don't think that's always a failing.' Dagrappi lit the cigar which Russell offered. 'So we'd been keeping a discreet eye on you and as it happened we came in useful. Not that the men who attacked you were more than hired hoodlums. They were very poor stuff indeed. They couldn't even hold their tongues.'

'I'm assuming the others were friends of yours. What did the first two tell them?'

'Everything, and disgracefully quickly. The idea was to snatch you and to hold you in a farm near Bergamo till Friday.'

'Till everything was over? Till the *Rose* had been launched or a strike had prevented the launching?'

'Presumably. They hadn't been trusted with much of the background, but they admitted who'd hired them and I'm sure he's not a principal. There'd be another behind him before we touched even that consulate, and behind that again there's our Luthman.' Renato Dagrappi shook his head. 'No, a line through those louts wouldn't help us. So I'll tell you what I've done and then we'll think. First I've taken those two stooges and I've hidden them.'

Russell nodded approvingly but he didn't ask where. Nor would Dagrappi have told him. This was another private joke which he couldn't share. The two men were hidden, guarded, in Mario Donnini's Rapallo flat. There were disadvantages in having a cousin as Commissario of Police, but when the cousin-Commissario had a discreet country hide-out there were clearly advantages too. That Mario Donnini owned this flat was convenient insurance if something by chance went wrong, since the Commissario wouldn't wish to explain why a man called Dagrappi had the key of his seaside apartment. An eminent communist called Dagrappi, Donnini's cousin. . . . It had really been rather neat, he thought, Sicilian in its elegance. It had tickled his sense of humour and still amused him. He suppressed a laugh but allowed a smile, resuming his explanation.

'So firstly we've taken those clowns away, and secondly we've been busy up at Bergamo. There were a farmer and his wife but they gave us no trouble. To a Bergamasco peasant our money's as good as Luthman's, so they obligingly did some telephoning. They rang back to Vittorio, reporting the safe arrival of Colonel Charles Russell and escort. That titbit will go to Massaro no doubt, and in time to Carl Luthman too. They'll both think you're snug at Bergamo, they'll both think the plan succeeded.'

Charles Russell was impressed but he'd been trained to think of detail. 'Those men left a car outside.'

'That hadn't escaped me, we took it away.'

Russell said respectfully: 'You really think of everything.'

'Not quite of everything and that's why I'm here. Luthman will think that you're out of the way, so you've an option if you want it.'

'An option to lie low a bit?'

'I thought you might like to think of it.'

Charles Russell began to do so, smoking unhurriedly. He had indeed an option and it was one which strongly tempted him. If you looked at it in principle it was an advantage to let your enemy believe he had eliminated you when in fact he had done no such thing, and in practice if Russell emerged again, let it be known that he hadn't been kidnapped, there was always the chance that they'd go for him again. He thought it a slim one but he'd caused trouble enough already, and he'd look the idiot of all time if a second attempt succeeded. Yes, there were advantages in lying low in via Vanda. He returned to Dagrappi.

'You've handled this extremely well. If you ever decide to change sides, if ever you want a job . . .'

Renato bowed.

'But there are one or two loose ends still. My hotel, for instance.'

'I could look after that.'

'I'd be grateful if you would. Indirectly would be better since we shouldn't risk Luthman hearing there's a link between you and me. But I've a man of my own here called Bailey.' Russell wrote an address down. 'I had money when I arrived last night and I'm told that it's now in the safe. Please take it and give it to Bailey. He's to settle my bill and send my luggage back to London. If Luthman should happen to hear of that he'll deduce I've been missed but that my people are covering up until they find me. And that would be exactly what they'd do. Tomorrow looks like crisis day and I can live with what I've got till then. But if you could buy me a razor, a toothbrush and another shirt——'

Dagrappi produced a parcel from his briefcase. 'Add some odd-ments and it's all in there.'

'I was serious about that job.'

Renato laughed. 'You really mustn't tempt me. And talking of the Executive, that's another loose end.'

'Not for long—I mean to ring them. They've been sending me a courier daily but I'll cancel that at once. And may I give them your number in case anything genuinely important breaks in London?'

'*My* number?'

'Hardly this one.'

Renato's face didn't change but again he could have laughed aloud. The head of the Executive holed-up in Vittorio's cat-house. It wouldn't count in London that that wasn't what it was. They wouldn't understand at all, Charles Russell might barely survive it.

But he was speaking again. 'That leaves Neil Stoddart and Donnini as the other two people to think of. How much should they know, if anything? I'd be grateful for your advice, you know.'

A compliment had been intended and was accepted as gracefully. 'Neil Stoddart ought to know, I think, or at least have the means of knowing. Would you be agreeable to something like this? I could tell him that you've good reasons to disappear until tomorrow, but that if he really needs to contact you I can bring him to where you are.'

Russell nodded. 'And Donnini?'

'Are there positive advantages in telling him?'

'There are positive disadvantages.' Colonel Russell was emphatic. 'We can't prevent his being curious when he discovers I've left the Manin, he may even suspect I've some plan to embarrass him. But if he rings the Executive they won't tell him a thing, and I doubt if he'll start inquiries in Vittorio simply because my luggage was sent to London.'

'And after all you're Charles Russell.'

'And in my own impoverished language this is a brothel.'

Renato said easily: 'I ought to confess I'd thought of that.'

'But had far too much tact to mention it.' Renato rose smiling and walked to the door. As he reached it Charles Russell stopped him. 'I'd forgotten one thing about not telling Donnini. You'll remember that he was keeping me in touch with Luthman's movements.'

'Thank you for reminding me—I'll take that over myself. May I call again this evening?' With his first hint of irony Dagrappi added smoothly: 'Meanwhile you're in very good hands.'

*

The Commissario Mario Donnini was pacing his room in the *questura*. He had just had an interview, and he couldn't remember another which had embarrassed him more acutely since the visit of Fred Adams. And Marco Monti wasn't comparable with Fred Adams. Fred Adams was an English queer, and though he had powerful friends the Commissario had a weapon in a pinch. Against Marco Monti he had none. His name assured that, he was unquestionably of the Family, and, more important, his position in the hierarchy was high. Donnini knew well that only good Montis had work at SAGA, and Marco had work which mattered. He was close to the Professor, he was in fact head contact man. When there was trouble and often there was then Marco Monti shot it. Political trouble especially.

He had come into Mario's office assured to the point of arrogance, not a bully since that seldom paid in Italy, but perfectly aware of his position and of Donnini's. He had stated the latter remorselessly. There'd been increasing trouble at SAGA, and Donnini was much too intelligent to accept that it could be explained as a series of coincidences. Even if he did so there were plenty who would not. Tiresome Roman officials were almost certainly doubtful already, and if the Commissario were to press him he'd have to admit he knew they were.

Marco Monti changed gear smoothly. Not, he said easily, that either of them need think twice about Roman officials. Both were good Vittorians, one by birth, the other adopted, and their opinions of the regrettable farce which posed as government from the centre would be identical. It therefore wasn't relevant that a series of outrages at SAGA had so far produced no arrests at all, nor that as his uncle the Professor saw it there wasn't the ghost of a guarantee that there wouldn't be further outrage. All that was of low importance because any sensible Vittorian would rather trust his Commissario than some half-baked Roman bureaucrat with a laureat in literature worth a pound or two a week. So if the Commissario chose to play this long no doubt he had good reason to. They could even be private reasons without a Vittorian getting nosy. One closed the ranks against Roman pigs; one always had and one always would. Vittorians understood each other.

Marco Monti's manner changed again. . . . And that was the point, since mutual understanding implied mutual obligation too. The Family was aware of theirs—they'd never go squealing to men they despised, they'd never complain behind a competent policeman's back.

They wouldn't, that is, just so long as he played along with them.

Mario Donnini had listened in silence, conscious that words were useless. He was being given instructions and they were very clear indeed. There was the chance of a strike at SAGA, and if it came it was to be broken. *Broken.*

When Monti had gone Donnini swore. It could still be done— the riot squads, the *celeri*, a calculated brutality with its roots from before the war. Donnini wasn't easily shocked but now he was shaken badly. The politics didn't interest him but the Montis might be miscalculating. The riot squads hadn't been used in force since

155

the early nineteen-fifties. They were useful still in tough patrols into areas even tougher, but to use them at this date punitively, night sticks and iron-shod poles like Indian police, rifle butts and brutal boots. . . .

The thing was an anachronism, the Montis had gone collectively mad. Donnini sighed for he knew they hadn't. With unemployment rising, with the bubble drifting down again, a strike would be invitation to a bigger, severer showdown. It made sense of a sort, it made Monti sense. It made Monti sense or they wouldn't be risking it.

Not to the Commissario. Ten years ago and politically it would have been possible, something to be represented as a necessary suppression of violence against a people with a taste for it, a country raped half silly by a war it had somehow lost twice. Today it would mean a serious riot, the Montis were miscalculating.

But were they? he thought grimly—they weren't the type. The question he put behind him for a decision wouldn't help him. *They'd* decided and they held him cold. . . . A major riot, a splash in all the newspapers, a cry for his blood from every party but one and that one he couldn't be sure of. That was one of his choices, the other worse. It was a cry for his blood in any case if the Montis chose to raise one. There'd been a bombing in SAGA and then a fire, not a single arrest since he hadn't dared make one. And that would be the end of him, the other only might be. He might ride it out, just conceivably he might ride it.

It occurred to him that he could always resign. He wouldn't be comfortable but he still had some land in Sicily. It was waterless and half derelict but he'd raise capital on his pension.

. . . Useless, today was Wednesday. They could hardly relieve him in much less than a fortnight, nor would the Montis accept resigning as a get-out. If he failed them they'd revenge themselves, and an ill-timed resignation would make it that much easier. The Commissario sighed again. It went against the grain to ask for help, especially from a foreigner like Charles Russell. He'd stupidly underestimated what had looked like a stage Englishman, but in a sense they had an alliance now. Russell might help him—must. He was powerful, that man, as well as clever.

Donnini went back to his desk, telephoning to the Manin, . . . Colonel Charles Russell? But he'd left the night before without leaving an address. Another Englishman had paid his bill and his bags had been flown to London.

Mario Donnini swore again. He rang off from the Manin to another number. He began to give orders, listening almost with detachment to the words as he spilled them out. He hated every one of them.

*

It was six o'clock when Renato Dagrappi returned to via Vanda. The doctor had vetoed alcohol, but Russell had wheedled a modest whisky. An active man, he was enjoying the rare luxury of having nothing whatever to do. Renato Dagrappi looked tired and strained, but said briskly: 'I've two pieces of news. First, I've talked to Neil Stoddart and I told him what you authorized me to say. He said that he wanted to see you tomorrow morning.'

'But the opening's at half-past eleven and his father will be arriving by the train which gets in at ten. He must be rushed off his feet.'

'He is—today especially. But he insisted he ought to see you. Would at eight be too early?'

'No. And your second piece of news?'

'I said we'd keep an eye on Luthman since you wouldn't be getting his movements from the Commissario. There've been developments.'

'Yes?'

'Luthman's been to his bank and drawn money in cash.'

'Have you any idea how much?'

'As it happens we've friends there. He drew ten million lire.'
'That's nearly six thousand pounds.'
'I know.'
'Here we go,' Russell said.

Chapter Fifteen

Pasquale Massaro got up early that Thursday morning. A new plan had been necessary and for ten million lire he'd made one. It had been several weeks since Carl Luthman had first contacted him, the original proposal that he throw his considerable weight behind calling an orthodox strike. The proposition had interested him but he hadn't considered it one to rush. For that matter neither had Luthman to begin with, and Pasquale Massaro, who hadn't been blind to later events, had very soon realized that a strike had been Luthman's backstop, not the weapon he thought of as his first. Had been—now wasn't: Luthman now wanted a strike at once and that was a different kettle.

Pasquale had weighed it carefully. He had been tempted by the first idea but had never been wholly sold on it. An orthodox strike would be an exercise in power, and if he forced it through and it were fought successfully it would leave him in unchallenged control of the union he was supposed to serve; he'd be Massaro of the metalworkers, a big shot, *the* Massaro, a man to reckon with in the politics of Vittorio. Carl Luthman would have paid him too, though not to the tune of ten million lire.

And now Luthman was clearly desperate, Massaro's decision as clearly different, for an immediate walk-out on a particular day wasn't something which could be guaranteed by making a rousing speech and waving a flag. On the other hand the unrest was there, the discontent, the powder. And it was Latin powder too, the flashpoint high. If he could somehow stir their sympathies, get them angry and excited. . . .

Pasquale, a Latin, had balanced the pros and cons. He'd been rising steadily in his union, and a successful orthodox strike would have left him on top of the pile. But he had asked himself what pile? for he wasn't stupid. The communists were infiltrating and Massaro's private terror was that the future lay with them. Which meant that he wouldn't have one since he wouldn't last five minutes once they achieved a straight majority. That mightn't be tomorrow but it could come.

In a changed situation the first and obvious move had been to squeeze a higher price from a frightened Swede. Luthman was desperate, Massaro was not, and that was a position which it would be foolish not to exploit. So it stood at ten million lire now, half paid already, half payable on completion. That was a respectable sum, more than attractive as an insurance against a future he wasn't sure of. It was a bird in the hand and he'd decided to settle for it. Despite the risks.

He'd known they were real ones, the worst that English Colonel. Pasquale had genuinely feared him more than the local police. His ideas about the Executive would have made Charles Russell laugh, but they'd been held quite sincerely and they'd been useful against Carl Luthman. . . . That terrifying Executive was somehow mixed up in SAGA, which implied that the risks had multiplied, which implied that the price must too. Pasquale had been adamant: indeed no price would tempt him while Colonel Charles Russell was still in Vittorio. It had been bargaining counter but solid truth too.

And it seemed that Carl Luthman had somehow succeeded.

Massaro had given him perhaps one chance in four—the Executive was powerful but he knew that Carl Luthman had connections of his own and in particular he'd made his guess at who finally stood behind him. So between them they'd somehow worked it: Charles Russell had disappeared, his luggage gone. Pasquale had asked no questions but he'd checked and he was satisfied. Colonel Russell had left Vittorio, and he'd hardly have done that to oblige Carl Luthman.

. . . The plan was on, a skilled man could do it.

Pasquale Massaro rose early, bicycling to SAGA, walking to a machine shop, one of three he was responsible for. It was deserted in the hours between the night shift and the day, the lighting off, eerie in the half dark. He looked down the lines of silent machines. . . . Fourth row, the last but two. It was the latest thing from Sweden and somewhat flashily engineered, but somewhere there'd been a bug in it. It had broken down twice and the insulation was suspect. One or two men had had minor shocks. The electricians had claimed to have found the fault, but it wasn't the present state of the machine which interested Pasquale: it was its past, its history.

In practice his cover.

He walked down the fourth row to the last machine but two. The workshop was unnaturally quiet, a cave in a half-world, not land, not sea. He put on a pair of rubber gloves. He had tools in his pocket and he began to use them quickly. One didn't become a supervisor at SAGA without a genuine expertise. When he'd finished he stood back. It might cost a man's life, but in Italy lives came cheaper than ten million.

He walked deliberately to his office and sat down. He had ample excuse to be there, even so early. It was going to be a big, big day.

It was, he thought—it was indeed.

★

Russell too had risen early to keep his appointment with Neil Stoddart, receiving him with reluctance and because he believed he must. But about one thing he needn't have worried. Neil was preoccupied and he'd never been observant. Evidently via Vanda wasn't a port of call of his, and he'd looked round the room with an air which suggested that he found it a little luxurious for the nursing home he assumed it was. Russell had taken an opening, murmuring blandly about an accident. He'd had a stupid little accident but he'd be quite all right for the launching at half eleven.

Ah, the launching—there was nothing new. Russell hadn't expected there would be, but such help as he could give he offered gladly. It wasn't a lot but he'd been telephoning to Sir Duncan, and he'd arranged that he should meet him on the train which arrived at ten. Neil Stoddart had been grateful: he'd have to be everywhere and his father could be demanding. He'd been telephoning himself, briefing Sir Duncan on the possibility of a strike, that the Montis were sticking their toes in against normal negotiations. Sir Duncan had been furious, for a great deal of Stoddart money was sunk in the *Princess Rose*. But he hadn't only been angry, and though far from explicit it had been Neil's impression that if the Montis put Stoddart interests last they wouldn't find him weaponless. The old man had a card and he'd play it when the time came. All that was in the future, though. For the present there'd been that meeting with the metalworkers the day before yesterday, but the new chairman Neil had spoken of had sat as pat as a Russian general with troops there first.

Neil had looked at his watch and left. The interview hadn't been fruitful and Russell had seen it end without regret. He had eaten already but he rang for more coffee when Neil had gone, smiling a little wryly. For he knew what he'd have to do if this were London not Vittorio: he'd call a conference of all concerned— Dagrappi, Neil Stoddart, Donnini, himself. But this being Italy, the affair having developed into the classic Italian free-for-all, that was out of the question. It was also out of the question that the head of the Executive should hold a conference in via Vanda. Not, he decided, that its absence was a disaster. Snatches of talk came back to him, 'on balance', 'marginally', 'putting out a marker', all the fashionable clichés of the current Whitehall jargon. A conference was no great loss.

But there was one thing he could do still, for Neil Stoddart had mentioned a matter he hadn't known. Perhaps she should have deduced it but he hadn't. Any strike must be a wild-cat since there wasn't the time for a formal one. There was machinery here for formal strikes and they enforced it pretty strictly, though on this day of all days a wild-cat would be as damaging. Russell rang the number which Renato Dagrappi had given him. A strange voice answered. Renato was busy and the Colonel would understand it, but he'd left another number. Charles Russell wrote it down and tried again. This time he was successful. He was at leisure himself until ten o'clock but he knew that Renato would not be.

'How goes it?'

'No betting.'

'There's one thing I learnt from Stoddart when he came to me this morning. A strike can't be a formal one—there isn't time to call it.' Russell added in apology: 'I dare say I should have thought of that and I'm perfectly sure that you have.'

'Oh yes. And it helps.'

'That tap on the head made me stupider than usual.'

Dagrappi, it seemed, had a moment to spare, or perhaps he was simply courteous. 'You remember that I dragged you on a sort of conducted tour?'

'And I thought I received your message loud and clear. You didn't control the unions but you controlled a lot of people.'

'Then you'll see how that helps us. We couldn't prevent a formal strike, but if there's walk-out we've a very fair chance to smother it. *If* there's a walk-out.'

'You mean you're not sure there will be?'

'Well, look at it as Massaro would. He's got a union in his pocket, or if that isn't quite true it's true enough, and with things as they are he could have swayed them into an orthodox strike—in time. But time is what he hasn't got—not for ten million lire. A strike along the rails would have cost much less.'

'I'd wondered myself,' Charles Russell said.

'Then I'm probably thinking sensibly. Luthman's playing it for the great big scene, and that means a flop at the opening today. Which calls in turn for a wild-cat strike, and I don't mean to be offensive in reminding you that there's no tradition here that a shop steward can call his shop out because the canteen tea was cold. Massaro can't say "Follow me", because it's better than even money that they'd just laugh at him and refuse. No, Pasquale has got to pull one, something to stir them, something emotional. You know what we Italians are.'

'Such as what?'

'If you'll tell me that I'll be greatly obliged.'

'And if Pasquale does pull something?'

'I said we'd have a chance to get them back. We've plenty of party members already employed in SAGA, and I've slipped in some more with connections and really trusted. Come to think of it, you've met four of them. And I'm here myself for what that's worth.'

'You're inside SAGA now, on a SAGA number?'

'Both correct.'

'You're my boy,' Russell said.

'I'm your boy for the moment, your limited boy.'

'And you really think you could ease them back if Pasquale does bring them out?'

'I told you—no betting.'

'On what you very kindly showed me I'd bet rather a lot.'

'You shouldn't you know—you'd be betting blind. We're not a

cold-blooded people. It would only need a little thing, some foolishness, some arrogance . . . Once out we couldn't hold them then.'

'A foolishness by whom?'

'I wish I knew that.'

*

The Commissario Mario Donnini was giving orders again, and they were orders which his cousin Renato would have described by a single word. He had used it to Russell and he'd have used it again. Mario Donnini was committing a foolishness. He was telephoning to Vittorio's biggest hospital. They'd be wise to have Casualties at something more than normal strength, and if things turned really ugly there'd be a call for beds as well. . . . How many beds? Play it safe and say thirty.

He put down the telephone, hating Mario Donnini. He had never been conditioned in favour of strikers as such: enthusiasm in that context was adolescent—one had only to look at the enthusiasts. But though a policeman he was still a man, and a cold-blooded beat-up shocked him. If strikers got out of hand that would be one thing; that would be a duty and he'd accept it; but being blackmailed by the Monti clan. . . . He walked to the window and spat out of it comprehensively. If he'd had only a little money he'd have spat in those prosperous faces. It wouldn't have done much good, of course. There were plenty of other policemen who'd like his job.

He went to the lavatory, compulsively washing his hands. Once back in his room he almost wept. Well, he thought grimly, they'd be rougher in Palermo.

Chapter Sixteen

Russell met Sir Duncan Stoddart's train at ten o'clock. Sir Duncan always slept well on trains, and he climbed down the steps of the *wagon lit* looking a good deal fitter than Russell had expected, an elderly charger excited by scent of battle. And for battle he had prepared himself.

In the car up to SAGA Sir Duncan chuckled. That Neil of his was a sensible boy and he'd realize the importance of having more to show a buyer than a single *Princess Rose*. Just the same he thought first of flying her. That was natural, even praiseworthy. Neil's business was to produce the *Rose* but Sir Duncan's was to sell her, and if Neil had been talking about showing her paces, well, she'd do so no doubt, but it wouldn't be the main thing. Hard-boiled buyers of aircraft didn't order on a fly-around, and the occasion today was exceptional. Because so were the circumstances, the delays and the sabotage. People would want to see the *Rose*, but they'd be even more interested in what they could see behind her. Her potential and her performance were well known, even the smear campaign hadn't wholly destroyed the facts, but delays were a different matter. These buyers must see *production*. Sir Duncan had been insistent on that, so the plant was to be working and the plant was to be wide open. Half the buyers would give the *Rose* a cheer, then fade away; they'd fade to the shops and assembly sheds, and they were very well qualified to draw conclusions from what they saw. They were certainly well enough qualified to notice if there were a strike on. Had Russell the latest news on that?

'I saw Neil earlier this morning. He was worried but nothing's broken yet.'

'That's good—for the moment.'

'Neil's been keeping you in the picture about the Montis?'

'You're thinking about a *future* strike, something the Montis might invite because they wanted one?' Sir Duncan lit a cigarette, one of the ten his doctors allowed him; he said firmly: 'I've got that fixed.'

'You've a seat on the main board?'

'Of course I haven't. They offered me one but I turned it down. You don't control a gang of slippery wops by being in a minority of one in the boardroom. You control them by having a gun at their heads. I've got one.'

Charles Russell was silent but not in disapproval. The Stoddart language was abrasive but the approach entirely valid. Russell might even learn from it. You didn't intrigue against Italian intrigue since native gifts made defeat quite certain. Instead you collected power and you laid it down. Charles Russell sighed inaudibly, conscious that in Vittorio he'd been dancing to a tune which he hadn't called. It hadn't been his fault perhaps, he'd been wholly without authority, but the experience had soured him. This endless, pointless machination, intrigue almost for its own sake, this gifted, impossible people . . .

He realized with some surprise that they'd spent his patience. If they leant on him today he wouldn't look for accommodation; he'd look for a weapon and he'd use anything which offered. Sir Duncan was right.

But he was talking again, saying calmly: 'I'll look after the

167

future, the Montis, that is. It's today which really bothers me. Today is immediate crisis.'

They were nearing SAGA, driving alongside the high wire fence. At the gatehouse there was a more careful than usual check, then they were slipping along the central artery. Sir Duncan had nodded but he raised his head suddenly. 'There's been trouble,' he said softly, 'and it's still going on.'

'How do you know?'

'Damn it, Charles, I do know. Once I worked for a wage, but I've been employing men for forty years. I know there's trouble in a plant before I see it.'

'You're sure?'

'I smell it,' Sir Duncan Stoddart said.

*

He was a skilled machinist, not pleased at having to work on this of all days. It wasn't a national holiday and there was no good reason why he shouldn't be working a normal stint, but he would have preferred to watch the festivities. So would most of his friends. They'd been assured that festivities was quite the wrong word for a visit by sober buyers, but a certain resentment remained and rankled. There had even been talk in the union about a strike, but a man called Massaro had been by far the loudest talker and the machinist distrusted him profoundly. He was a man from the *mezzogiorno* who'd arrived in Vittorio with two bags and the clothes he stood in, and he'd bettered himself the hard way, learning a trade. His political party had helped him, for his politics he'd brought with him. They weren't particularly logical but at least they were clear on one point: he belonged to his union since there'd be difficulties if he didn't, but when a man like Massaro was breathing fire about a sudden strike—look out! He was a first-class hand and devoted to his family. His party had helped them too, still did—his flat, his taxes, even lodgings for his holidays. He was typical of the grassroots where Dagrappi's party flourished.

So he was glad there was no silly strike but he'd come to work reluctantly. The wine mightn't be flowing and there wouldn't be fireworks, but it would have been pleasant to watch the foreigners. The local brass too, though he hated their well-fed guts. In the end there'd been a compromise: there'd be a single shift from half-past ten till two, and when it had served its purpose, which they'd explained to him was publicity, they could go. Time-and-a-half and a half day off. It hadn't seemed unreasonable, and like every good southerner he had reason behind the apparent foam and froth.

He went to his locker and changed his clothes, then walked to his Swedish machine. On the wooden bench beside it there was a pile of waiting sheet steel, rather less, he noticed happily, than would normally take him three hours and a half. He put a sheet on the machine-table and adjusted the jig and cutter. He then threw the switch.

His back arched like a bow but he didn't make a sound. He fell clear of his machine. Somewhere there was a muffled bang as the shop's main fuse blew noisily. Then a terrifying silence—the shop was dead. So was the skilled machinist.

For an instant nothing happened, then there was pandemonium.

*

Russell and Sir Duncan Stoddart drove on till a barrier stopped them. A man was flagging the car to the right down a feeder road, the main hangar now to the left of them. They stopped in an improvised car park and Charles Russell looked around him. If they'd driven past the barrier they'd have come to the wrecks of the paintshop and the offices, an untidy jumble of shacks and caravans. Now the hangar hid the skeletons and Russell nodded approvingly. It had been admirably arranged but Neil was competent. The side of the main hangar nearest them had been stripped from the steelwork which held the roof, and the *Rose* was fully visible. In front of her lay the runway, broadening into a network of turning points and lay-bys, fading finally into neglected fields. To the right was another hangar, slightly staggered from the *Rose*'s, and a workshop behind them was third wall to an asphalt stage. There were adequate but casual chairs, but the setting hadn't been furnished as a forum. The speeches would come later, in SAGA's boardroom and in hotels. It wouldn't look odd to leave your seat, supposing you ever took one. There would be no introductions here, no formality, no restrictions. It was open house and so intended.

And on the tarmac between the buildings there was a press of milling men. There were two hundred perhaps, but the number was growing steadily, little knots running in through the gaps between the buildings, a chorus crowding the arena through a theatre's classic entrances. There was the smell of excitement, palpable to the senses—excitement but anger too. Somewhere there was the clamour of an ambulance's bell. The tension rose.

Sir Duncan sat down on an uncomfortable chair, watching the scene inscrutably. His hooded old eyes were very blue. He said astonishingly calmly:

'So it's happened.'

Russell was aware that Dagrappi was standing beside him. Renato touched his sleeve. 'If we could have a private word.'

'Of course.'

'A man has been killed—electrocuted. He was a friend of mine but we'll consider that later. His machine had given trouble twice before. The men aren't pleased.'

'Pasquale Massaro?'

'I think so. I've found out he came early and the machine shop was one of his. He'd know the machine's back history.'

'You told me he'd have to pull something.'

'So he has and still is. Look over there.'

Russell had brought binoculars and he swung them where Renato pointed. Pasquale Massaro was standing on two chairs, making a speech, gesticulating, frenetic. But he wasn't the only focus and Russell's instinct was that he knew it. There were other groups too, much quieter, still undecided, but centred again on a single man. Russell adjusted the glasses. They were thick-set dark men in square-ish suits and Russell had met two of them. One was the porter of a working-class block of flats, the other ran a restaurant. He turned to Renato.

'Your friends, I see.'

'And with a fifty-fifty chance, I'd say. We're not trying to stop the protest—this is Italy and they're human—but we're pulling out every stop to kill a strike.' Dagrappi smiled dourly. 'You'll observe that Massaro takes the opposite view. But I've a hope we can hold them. They trust us, they don't trust him. We should hold them barring accidents.'

'What accidents?'

'I wish I knew. Something wholly unexpected. A—a foolishness.'

'I'd like you to meet Sir Duncan,' Charles Russell said. He led Dagrappi to where Sir Duncan sat. Neil Stoddart had joined him. Sir Duncan was saying, still massively matter-of-fact: 'The first of our visitors may be arriving about eleven for half past.' He pulled out an ancient watch, consulting it. 'It's now half-past ten so you've exactly half an hour.'

Neil Stoddart didn't answer him.

Russell said formally: 'I present Renato Dagrappi. He's a communist big shot and a very good friend of mine. He's also on our side, at least today.'

Sir Duncan Stoddart rose, shook hands. 'Delighted,' he said. He sat down again deliberately and Russell gave him alpha plus. It wasn't every tycoon who took so calmly to a communist. Charles Russell began to explain but Stoddart stopped him.

'I've had the outlines from my son. There's been an industrial accident, I'm sorry to say a fatal one, and that man on the chairs is trying to turn a protest into a walk-out. He's not doing badly but I'd noticed there's competition.' Sir Duncan's blue eyes turned alertly on Dagrappi. 'I now gather that you're the competitor. This isn't the moment for questions about your motives. Just let me thank you.'

But Dagrappi was staring at the excited men. They'd gone suddenly quiet, and where there'd been separate groups there was now one big one. They moved silently, like animals forming instinctive herd, protecting themselves in numbers, unthinking mass.

Renato had frozen, raising a rigid arm. In the open space beyond the right-hand hangar something was happening. Russell watched it, incredulous. There were half a dozen jeeps and behind them what looked like fire-engines. Men were already dismounting, coupling high-pressure hoses. Behind the engines again were two loads of lorried infantry. The word had been a reflex though Russell knew it to be the wrong one. These men weren't troops but policemen. He saw very little difference. All were steel-helmeted, in something like battle order; all moved with a disciplined menace.

. . . The riot squads, the hated.

Russell, staring through his glasses, altered focus. Mario Donnini was sitting in the central jeep, and he was in uniform and armed. Charles Russell put his glasses down.

'The bloody fool.'

He had spoken aloud but he didn't hear his words. The men on the tarmac were a single solid mass by now and they'd given a sort of collective groan. Fists had risen instinctively, not always in party salute. They shook in a second's silence and Russell waited. He

172

knew about crowds and he knew what was coming. It was a full-throated roar. There was rage in it and something more—defiance. Then the rhythmic chanting started. Russell caught the *Abbasso* but not the word which followed it. He was experienced with crowds and without knowing it he shivered.

Dagrappi was pulling his sleeve again; he said briefly: 'We've had it.'

*

They had to shout to make themselves heard—Russell, the Stoddarts, Dagrappi. Russell shouted at Sir Duncan: 'It's the Commissario who's leading them. I know him.'

'Then you've very stupid friends as well as good ones.'

'I might try to make him see sense.'

'With what weapon in your hand, please?'

'I don't think I have one.'

Renato said unhappily: 'I have.'

'Then we'd all of us be grateful.'

Dagrappi didn't answer but sat down. His face was grey, he was torn in two. He was as dedicated to his communism as a priest to his daily altar and the interests of his party were both plain and inescapable. . . . Stop this strike and stop this beat-up. And he could do it, he had the tool. The Commissario was his cousin and he wouldn't last a day once that were known. Of course he wouldn't have brought the riot squads in without very clear orders to use them, and it was usually pretty dangerous if you flatly ignored your orders. Dangerous, yes, but not invariably fatal. You might talk your way out of it and Donnini talked well. But what he couldn't talk his way from was common blood with a top flight communist.

Renato Dagrappi wrung muscular hands. The weapon was unthinkable, an outrage to race and blood. Blood was a glue, not a

173

card in a game of *scopa*. It held a family together in a shifting and hostile world; blood was sacred and unbetrayable.

And still he was a communist but not, it seemed, a good one.

He rose shakily and bowed. 'I was wrong,' he said quietly, 'I'm very sorry but I was wrong.'

'Then we've been wasting valuable minutes.' Sir Duncan was polite still but for the first time he was irritated. He looked at his watch again. 'It's a quarter to eleven and I see movement amongst those policemen.'

He was right, Russell saw. They had wheeled to the left, forming line against the chanting crowd. It was more angry than ever but it hadn't yet quite gone over. It was people still not a single unthinking beast. But when the noise dropped a tone or two. . . .

For the second time Russell shivered, looking at the police again. The jeeps were in front, then a line of men, then the high-pressure hoses and the last of the men behind them. The jeeps had double fenders and loose coils of barbed wire at the sides. It reminded Charles Russell of a rather old-fashioned tank battle, the sort where tanks fought men not tanks.

It might be old-fashioned but it terrified Russell.

Sir Duncan had turned to his son at his side. 'Have you any ideas?'

Neil shook his head.

'And you, Charles?'

'I think I'll talk to Donnini after all.'

'You've decided you've got a chance to show him sense?'

'Perhaps.'

Dagrappi said: 'I'll come with you.'

'No thank you—better not.' Charles Russell began to walk away. He had done some quick thinking but he wasn't by any means sure of it. His second name was Michael and he muttered a brief prayer to him.

*

He didn't attempt to pass through the chanting men, moving to the left of them, making a trotting cast through the *Rose*'s hangar. He was in enviable shape for his age and he trotted easily. As he saw it Donnini was frightened. Neil Stoddart had been explaining that the Montis might really want a strike, and they could only sensibly want a strike if they wanted it brutally broken. And they'd have plenty on Donnini to make him play—explosions, a fire, and all unexplained, a week's major crime and nothing whatever to show for it. That was how Russell saw it as he walked steadily towards the jeeps. It might not be a triumph for the modern deductive method but at least there was a chance it would be right. Charles Russell sincerely hoped so. If it were right he'd have a stick to beat Donnini, for a frightened man could be counter-frightened. But if he were wrong he'd look more foolish than he cared to.

Also, he thought grimly, there's be the bloodshed he detested.

Russell paced on, not hurrying but not lagging, halting at the central jeep, facing the astonished police. Between the policemen and the tight-packed crowd he felt extraordinarily lonely and exposed. It was an occasion for a salute, something formal, an acknowledgement. He couldn't salute in the clothes he wore but he'd decided how to handle it. He'd come the English Colonel and he'd lay it on thick. It wasn't a part he fancied but in a pinch he could play it convincingly. He snapped curtly, looking down the line: 'May I ask what the war's about?'

Mario Donnini ducked it. 'They told me you were in London,' he said.

'Then they told you quite wrong. I had reasons to disappear for a bit, but now I wish I hadn't. If I'd known about this non-sense——'

'But really . . .' Donnini sounded aggrieved. 'But this isn't *correct*, it really isn't. I'd hoped that our understanding——'

'Rubbish. Our understanding contained nothing about my

disappearing for thirty-six hours, far less finding you leading a beat-up.'

Donnini said: 'Careful.'

'But it's you to be careful. Get down and have a word with me.'

'I've nothing to say.'

'Get down off that jeep unless you want your men to hear me in Italian.' Donnini hesitated but got down, and Russell lowered his barrack-square bark into something more like his normal tone. 'Now please listen carefully. I've had certain information and I reckon I've made the deductions. You've been ordered to use violence and you intend to obey your orders.' He looked at Donnini squarely. 'You're the stooge,' he said.

'I'm under very great pressure, you're right about that.'

'It's the time to use your head, you know.'

'It's not my fault.'

'Whose is it?'

'Fate's.'

Charles Russell swallowed. He'd been playing the English Colonel but now he was near to being one. . . . Italians—he was sick of them. There was something called Latin realism but in practice it didn't exist. They got themselves in muddles and they deserved to. Then they blamed fate. Their passion for intrigue, an almost compulsive deviousness. . . . One mustn't be sanctimonious since in a way there was worse in England, jobs for the boys, a horde of alien pundits in lush work which they couldn't handle. It was corruption, offensive, but at least it had an object. Here trickiness was endemic, a disease of the blood and horrible. If they'd only go straight for five minutes a day. . . .

Unhappily they couldn't; they complicated the simplest thing, then complained when the backwash caught them; they left reluctant Englishmen holding babies they hadn't fathered. Charles Russell looked round at the crowd again. There'd been an indefinable change in it. The chanting was going on still but the rhythm had slightly slowed. One or two men had knelt in prayer. The tiniest push, a nothing, and the crowd would be a raving mob. Charles Russell knew. It might break like chaff as the butts came down or it might tear some shrieking policeman limb from limb. Barehanded, oblivious—a riot. In which case there'd be shooting too, and Russell loathed shooting. He said quickly to Donnini: 'We've less time than you think, so hear me—I'm older. I've seen English riots and German, I've seen Spaniards and Indians too. Do you think these men are Indians? Do you think they'll stand there quietly while your men ride them down?'

'It's the least of the risks,' Donnini said stubbornly.

'You mean it's the least of your *personal* risks?'

The Commissario didn't answer and Charles Russell was ashamed for him. A little for himself as well. This dialogue wasn't displeasing, he was privately rather enjoying it, but it wasn't in fact a dialogue. There was a third and he turned his head again—people, a human presence. Or it was that by the thinnest thread still. The crowd had ominously quietened: more had joined them but they were compacter. Russell couldn't be sure of it but he thought they'd inched nearer. There was a faint smell of sweat in the wintry sun and something else as corporeal. It was hatred and Russell feared it.

He felt the fear for a second, then anger swamped it. . . . Away with this talky-talk, this stylized sparring between fellow officials. These were men and there'd be shooting. Charles Russell was experienced, he knew. He might mistrust moral judgements but he didn't mistrust his instincts. He was suddenly in a towering rage and in no way trying to rein it. He swung on Donnini, snarling.

'So a beat-up's the least of your personal risks? I'm going to change your mind for you. The first move you make and I'm going in there to join them. And I've friends here who will come with me.'

'You're mad.'

'That's your gamble, not mine, but it's worth a careful think about. . . . A man called Charles Russell with a certain reputation; the son of an English tycoon; a well-known communist——'

'Which communist?'

'What does it matter?' Charles Russell choked, recovered himself with difficulty. 'Quite a curious collection when the Press of the world descends on you. Why were they rioting? *Were* they rioting? Why are they in hospital or worse?'

'Because they mixed themselves up in what didn't concern them.'

'Don't be stupider than God made you. You think you can get away with that? Englishmen and a communist, all fighting the police for their lives at SAGA? Tell that to our Consul-General when he gets here.'

There was an oppressive silence, then the crowd began to shout again, deep-throated, human still, but balanced on a knife-edge. Russell gave it a minute, conscious that he was sweating too.

He hadn't noticed at once that another man had joined them. Mario Donnini was staring at him but Renato didn't speak. He put his arm through Russell's with a gesture of utter simplicity, standing level with him, expressionless. The message was inescapable, the threat, to a policeman, limitless.

Donnini had flushed but his face, now, was bloodless. His lips were in labour with frightful words but no sound escaped them. He raised his arms and let them fall, then he turned on his heel deliberately. He walked to his jeep, fumbling for his whistle. On it he blew three short blasts, one long. The jeeps gunned their engines and turned away.

Renato Dagrappi took Russell's hand. He tried to pull it free but Renato held. They walked towards the waiting crowd. Behind was the noise of an orderly retreat but the crowd had gone silent, watching them. Six feet from the front rank Renato stopped. He said something in dialect and raised Russell's arm. For an instant nothing happened, then there was a sort of sigh, an enormous explosive laugh of sheer relief. The crowd parted and they walked through it. Most were clapping and cheering but some of them were weeping. Colonel Charles Russell was trying not to.

*

When they came to Sir Duncan the crowd was still cheering but it had begun to melt away again, vanishing as it had come, in little groups but laughing now, or silently in deliverance. Dagrappi said: 'They'll go back to work now, there's nothing else to do. They've won. We can cut the broken machine out too—the rest of that shop will be working with the others.'

Sir Duncan began to speak but Renato stopped him. 'Perhaps later,' he said politely, 'but now I've work.' He looked at Charles Russell, his face like a stone. 'A friend of mine died——'

'I understand.'

'There's a bottle in my bag,' Sir Duncan said.

They walked to the car park as the first black saloons came into it. Four sleekly-dressed men got out of them. One was a journalist and Neil Stoddart waved to him. Another was Carl Luthman and Russell stared. Luthman looked ill, at the end of his tether, and in success one could be generous. It occurred to Charles Russell to wish Luthman luck.

Not that it could help him now.

Chapter Seventeen

Charles Russell had been confident that if he returned to the Manin with a brown paper parcel and an air of exaggerated Englishness they wouldn't ask him for explanations. His confidence had been justified for the hotel was a good one, perfectly conditioned to male customers' sudden absences. They'd given him the same room again, and he'd woken next morning facing a day which would rush him. It needn't have done so since he could have tied up his ends at leisure, but he hadn't much taste for further chores in Vittorio and he'd booked on the midday plane. He reflected as he shaved that one end had been clewed already. The *Princess Rose* was safe. They'd averted a wild-cat yesterday and for the future there'd be no formal strike. Sir Duncan was perfectly sure of it.

Risking a nick, Charles Russell smiled. He'd have given much money to have been present at the interview between the Professor and Sir Duncan, but Sir Duncan had sketched the outlines as he'd climbed into his sleeper the night before and Russell could fill in the details from private knowledge of Sir Duncan. Who had indeed had the hand he'd hinted and had played it unhesitatingly. With four aces and a joker he'd even at first been reasonable. He could see, he'd said deceptively, that the Montis had other interests besides the *Rose* and that circumstances could arise, though personally he deplored them, in which other considerations might outweigh her. That was fair as a statement? Yes? Then the Professor mustn't take umbrage if a man in Sir Duncan's position, a man (this was putting it with charity) whose legitimate interests were on risks where he wasn't consulted took reasonable and prudent steps to cover the risks in question.

The Professor hadn't liked this much since he'd geared himself for protests about bad faith. He had listened silently, watching Sir Duncan. And it seemed to Sir Duncan that any strike should be avoided. Negotiations should be started and any reasonable wage increase paid. The market would bear it, the market must.

Must wasn't a word the Professor was used to and it had stung him to inquire acidly how Sir Duncan proposed to enforce his view.

By protecting his investment—they seemed to be agreed that this was prudent. If the Professor was interested . . .

He had been interested.

Sir Duncan had laid them smoothly down. He'd been telephoning to a friend of his, a Mr Garnett Anderson of Amalgamated Aircraft. The Professor would realize that friend was a modest euphemism, since Anderson had been doing his damnedest to destroy the *Rose*'s prospects. The negotiation had been delicate, but perhaps not as difficult as the outsider might imagine, for it was an essential of big business to change alliances when it was necessary. So Sir Duncan had reached an alternative arrangement with Mr Anderson. It would come into force the moment it was clear that the *Rose* had got stuck at SAGA, and an obviously avoidable strike would be interpreted as sticking. The designs of the *Rose* were SAGA's, the engines weren't, and Garnett Anderson would take them for what in effect would be a rival *Rose*. After all, Sir Duncan had come into Vittorio in the first place to find a market for his engines, and now that he was in any event assured of it. . . . The loss of the capital which his firm had sunk here in SAGA? Yes, that could be serious—he wasn't spoiling his case by overstating it —but Amalgamated's appetite for engines could be four or five times SAGA's, and though there'd be a loss at first he reckoned long term to take it. In any case he'd have to if the Professor forced him into it, and it wouldn't escape a business man that there wasn't another engine to suit the *Rose*. . . . Breach of contract, of solemn treaty?

For a moment Sir Duncan had been unregenerate Duncan Stoddart. Sue and be damned. What they'd distrain on if the case ever ended would be the plant which the Stoddarts had helped with. Much good might it do them engine-less.

Charles Russell put his razor away, able at last to laugh. Commercial morality had always fascinated him next to communist, and Renato Dagrappi was the first on his list of interviews. It had been agreed for eight-thirty and it was that as he finished dressing. He waited till ten to nine, then telephoned.

A woman's voice answered him, speaking Italian but evidently not. . . . Signor Dagrappi? The name was unknown. Russell apologized, then dialled again. This time he asked the number first, and after a second's hesitation it was admitted. Then Renato Dagrappi. . . ?'

There was some mistake. Kindly cease from troubling.

Charles Russell sat down, frowning and puzzled. Renato was courteous, he wouldn't break an appointment carelessly. Russell looked at his watch. His next engagement was with the Commissario and a taxi would take him to the *questura* in ten minutes. He had a moment to spare and he turned to the morning's newspapers.

They made interesting reading. Yesterday's function at SAGA was reported in all of them, the successful lunches and junketings afterwards, but there wasn't a hint that the occasion had dodged disaster by a hair's breadth. Charles Russell's frown melted. It was true that the Press hadn't been there when the story had actually broken, but you couldn't prevent men talking nor stop the nose of experienced journalists. No, this was calculated. Monti policies might be suspect but Press relations they managed admirably. Since they owned more than half of it that wouldn't be so difficult.

Russell picked up the one Independent, independent of tycoon interests. This was the paper of Renato Dagrappi's party, and Russell had made a private bet how this pompous party organ would be handling yesterday's story. One thing was certain: they'd be running it on the party line, either protest if they felt safe enough or total, disdainful ignorance of a capitalist extravagance. He saw at once that they'd chosen neither. What they carried was an obituary—black-edged photograph, all the trimmings. A man had been killed at SAGA, a party member in good standing, and a civilized law of libel permitted comment. He'd been electrocuted by a machine which had given trouble, and employers who allowed such things, their technicians, their supervisors. . . .

A tiresome political lecture followed but Russell didn't read it. Nor, for that matter, did many others. Vittorio wasn't the only town where a left wing daily bored the faithful leftwinger. He threw the paper on the bed and it opened around the middle page. There was a photograph of a street accident, the sort of thing which any Italian newspaper would use as a daily filler. Russell idly read the caption, then he read it again less idly. A man called Massaro, a supervisor at SAGA, had been returning home at half-past two; he'd been riding a bicycle and it seemed that he didn't often. He'd lost control and a truck had caught him. The driver (looking contrite) had told a straightforward story and there hadn't been any witnesses.

Charles Russell whistled softly. It clearly wasn't healthy to electrocute party members, but the speed of it, the effrontery . . .

He'd reflected once before about a state within a state, so a rule of law outside it shouldn't surprise him. An eye for an eye, the southern creed. Not despicable—inconvenient. Inconvenient for Charles Russell who had wished to thank Dagrappi before he left. From the picture in the newspaper Renato hadn't been killing personally, but he'd talked casually of removals when they'd been speaking of Carl Luthman, he'd dropped a public hint yesterday that killing his friends was dangerous, and he was known to the police as a power in his party. So he'd be wise to go underground for a while and evidently he'd done so. Russell wondered where he'd choose for it. Back in Sicily? No, hardly. He'd had a mission in Vittorio and he wasn't the type to quit on it. Charles Russell made a mental note. He'd have a drink on the aircraft and he'd drink to Renato Dagrappi.

He packed his brown paper parcel neatly, settling his bill for the second time. Then he sent for a taxi and directed it to the *questura*. It was an engagement he'd looked forward to—he had a request to make and this time some power behind it. That, he thought happily, would be an agreeable change from ten days of caballing which had riled and frustrated him. There was barb on his hook now as well as bait. Not that he need mention it—the Commissario was Italian.

Donnini received him coolly but entirely without resentment. A professional himself, he respected another, and he was aware of unfinished business which, if he mishandled it, could turn disastrously against him. He was certain Charles Russell would never job backwards—it would be the future which would concern him, not the past—and Russell's first sentence was precisely what he had hoped for.

'I've called about Carl Luthman,' Charles Russell said. He might have been inquiring about the weekly payment on the telly, and it was a note which Donnini was very happy indeed to echo. He said equally matter-of-factly: 'But we've an understanding about

Carl Luthman. We've had a recent, er, disagreement, but it didn't affect Mr Luthman. I undertook to keep you informed of him and I'm still prepared to do so.'

'I'm afraid I may want more than that.'

'*Ben inteso*. But let's start with the information just the same. In your unexplained absence, though I'm not asking for explanations, Luthman went to his bank. He drew money—ten million lire.'

'I know.'

'Then I congratulate you on your sources.' Donnini was ironical but still scrupulously polite. 'Still, perhaps I know more than you do. That ten million lire was drawn against an overdraft—secured, but only just. And we've been making some other inquiries too— one can, you know, in Italy. I'm not going to say that Carl Luthman's flat broke but he's lost a great deal of money somewhere. You know how a thing like that gets around, and moreover you'll see what it means.'

'I see what it means to you, my friend.'

He did indeed, Charles Russell thought. He had never believed Carl Luthman was simply a hired agent. A successful business man, he'd have gone in deeper—shares, God knew what. And with the *Princess Rose* assured again the wind could be blowing cold for him. That was one aspect but there was a second more important. Luthman had had protection and Charles Russell knew how protection worked. It was something you went on paying for, not something you laid down once for all. It wouldn't interest a protector that he'd pocketed large past sums. You paid your Danegeld regularly or you lost the advantage you sought to buy. And if you didn't have money. . . .

Donnini was trying to tell him that his hands were no longer tied. Come to that he was even saying so.

'If you've suggestions about Carl Luthman I'm free to listen.'

Russell batted it blandly back again. 'I'd be grateful for your advice.'

'Then we could rely on straightforward police work, start interesting ourselves in that damaged car——'

'Not good enough.'

'Or we could follow up on that ten million lire, though I don't think it would take us far. There'd be a consulate blocking the way to anything definite, and though I'm stuck with my local politics I deprecate trouble with diplomats.'

'Wisely. And so?'

'So I thought I'd just quietly run him out. He's still a foreign national, still here at our pleasure.'

'By bluff?' Russell asked.

'I might try bluff first but now we can act quite freely. And we've plenty of other methods if a quiet chat doesn't work for us.'

'So I've observed.' Charles Russell considered. 'So you'd deport him back to Sweden and you'd be ready to stand the fuss?'

'What fuss? He's a poor man now.'

Perhaps, Russell thought, he'd been wrong about Latin realism. This struck him as just, well meted, and he had far more faith in a policeman's idea of equity than in the pronouncements of formal courts. Luthman had once been rich, now wasn't; he'd lived his life for a single end and now that money had betrayed him he'd be rootless; he'd grown away from his own grim country which in any case hated failure. Send him back to Sweden and you'd be sending him into exile.

Some men preferred prison.

'Very well,' Russell said.

Yes, this was justice. Rather better than the other kind and very much quicker and cheaper. Call it penance or call it punishment, the words were the same to a civilized conscience.

Donnini was saying smoothly: 'I'm glad you agree since I've something to ask of you.'

Russell had expected it and he began to make it easy. 'We needn't speak about yesterday but you were talking about great pressure. I may be guessing wrongly but at least I've guessed the source of it.'

'You have?'

'I can't be quite sure.' Charles Russell made play with a cigarette, lighting his own and Mario Donnini's, adding casually across the flame: 'There'll be no strike at SAGA now. Instead they'll negotiate—pay.'

'You're sure?'

'Sir Duncan Stoddart is *perfectly* sure.'

'Then I needn't pursue it.' The Commissario rose, holding his hand out. 'You're an English official and there've been times when I've bitterly envied you. Now I'm almost a freeman myself. May I thank you——'

'Please don't.'

'To our next happy meeting, then.'

'To our next early meeting.'

There was a car outside and the driver saluted. 'I'm to take you to the airport, sir.'

'Very kind. Please stop at a florist's.'

Charles Russell ordered flowers for a lady, writing her a note as well. . . . There was an excellent air service between London and Vittorio and he intended to make good use of it. The note was more than a courtesy, something less than a firm decision. Via Vanda hadn't been an experience which at his age he had sought, but since it had imposed itself . . .

The head of the Executive liked to keep all his options open.

At the airport George Bailey joined him. Russell had wanted to thank him too. He'd been impressed by George Bailey and had plans for his advancement. If the balloon went up in Bonn again it would be just the place for a rising stringer. They weren't so easy to come by—not with sense. He had expected a certain formality but Bailey instead was bubbling. He gave Russell a sealed envelope and Russell read the contents.

'I'll have to think it over. I'll consider it and I'll let you know.'

They had a coffee at the airport bar, the last, Russell thought, before the depressing flood of tea engulfed him. Once on his aircraft he read Bailey's note again. Bailey had been excited and with good reason. He couldn't be quite sure and he'd duly check, but the source had been reliable. Mario Donnini, the Commissario of Police, was related and fairly closely to the communist boss Dagrappi.

Charles Russell was irritated. Ten days ago the information would have been invaluable, something to save him a voyage on seas he'd loathed, an unanswerable weapon against that tricky Commissario. He smiled unexpectedly. Tricky, he thought—poor devil, too. What sort of Commissario would Colonel Charles Russell make? Better? Improbable. Worse, just as shifty. . . ?

He remembered that he'd a toast to drink and he ordered a gin and tonic. Sherry on aircraft was always suspect. When it arrived he stirred most of the gas out. He drank the gin to Renato but he didn't include Donnini.

Instead he tore the note up small.